TOMORROW'S PROMISE

TOMORROW'S PROMISE

Women of the Ozarks

THE SCRAPBOOK SERIES, BOOK 1

NATALIE R. VICE

www.nataliervice.com

Felsenthal Publishing
Tuscaloosa, AL

Distributed by Bublish, Inc.

ISBN-13: 978-1-64704-150-2

CONTENTS

Women of the Ozarks
The Scrapbook Series

Memories of Tomorrow, A Prequel
Tomorrow's Promise
Crossing Yesterday
Unraveling
The Other Side
Wait For Me...

Discover more at
www.facebook.com/NatalierVice
www.natalievice.com

THIS BOOK IS DEDICATED to all the "gifters" of my life. When we arrive in life, we have been endowed by our Creator with talents, or gifts, as I like to call them. Each and every person is given a particular gift that provides them with the opportunity to contribute to the world in their own way. In my opinion, I have been blessed with many gifts. The greatest, however, is the gift of writing and communicating with my fellow travelers. As I sat down to write The Scrapbook Series, I thought about all the individuals who have "given" to me throughout my life, and helped to make it the wonderful collection of experiences I perceive it to be.

Thanks to everyone I've known and encountered. Because of you, I've experienced joy and sorrow, love and loss, success and failure, elation and despair--but most importantly, I've been given the chance to really live life. This book is dedicated to all of you. Thank you for the life that is my Scrapbook Series!

Sometimes life gives us magic, something that cannot be explained or reasoned, something or someone that changes the course of our life; call it luck, call it fate, or call it love. Families and true friends bring us magic moments that we collect and remember forever.

- Unknown

CHAPTER 1

1958 Polk Ridge
Jorja Felsenthal

THE WORLD THAT GREETED Jorja Ann was already in the midst of tremendous upheaval, thanks to the thousands of post-World War II babies that were now teenagers. Rock 'n' Roll had invaded the airwaves, old establishment rules were being broken, and the "peace and love" movement was ready to burst onto the scene. As Bob Dylan once said, "the times, they are a-changing."

Born to Tom and Maureen Felsenthal, Jorja was their second and last child and arrived in the spring. By the next spring, she was walking, and the following spring she was talking. The little girl with auburn hair and hazel eyes was the apple of her daddy's eye. Maybe because he had secretly longed for a boy and felt remorse for those thoughts; or it might have been because she favored her mother; or maybe because she reminded him of himself. Either way, he was extremely fond of his youngest daughter. And although she did resemble her momma, her actions and thoughts belonged to her daddy. As did the shortened version of her name, "Jo", he had bestowed upon her at birth.

Even as a small child, he took her to the co-op and spent many hours explaining why he loved his work. The co-op played an important role in the lives of farmers and residents of Polk Ridge, and Tom took pride in supporting their needs.

She very rarely chose to stay home with her mom and Stella, cooking and cleaning. She much preferred the musty, ancient building of the co-op or the mountains of her backyard to the laundry line or the kitchen sink. Her days usually divided between the mystery of the co-op and the magic of the mountains. She was surrounded by the majesty and allure of the Ozark Mountains.

Largely covered in green, and often shrouded in shadow, the foothills are the final traces of the Ozark Mountain chain. They more closely resemble small mountains, than actual rolling hills and those hills ran right up to the outskirts of town, framing the back of the Felsenthal house.

Her home, nestled among the last visible hill of the foothills, always reminded her of a watercolor painting. Color upon color that seemed to blend and run together to produce a picturesque setting.

Towering mountain peaks and grassy, wildflower-filled pastures would be the mental images she carried of home throughout her life. The mountains of her youth always called to her, whispering promises of mystery, excitement and freedom. Precious freedom.

Escape to the mountains meant freedom. Freedom to roam, explore and imagine. It was that feeling of freedom in those mountains that calmed and comforted her as she grew. No chores, no responsibilities, and no limits on her imagination. She could do anything when she escaped to the mountains.

Escape for Jo meant spending lazy days amongst tall white oaks, hickory and walnut trees with leaves and branches that formed a canopy of greens, creating a magical hiding place. A place where she would explore, hide and read.

Her favorite spot of course just happened to be only a few hundred yards from her house. A tangled mass of crape myrtle and honeysuckle that grew to encircle two giant white oaks and kiss the banks of the creek. Once you were behind the crape myrtle and honeysuckle, you entered another world. A world of shadows, cool breezes, sweet smells, and mystery.

The mingling smell of crape myrtles and honeysuckles filled every corner of her magic woods. It became a place to imagine that she was anywhere in time and space, anywhere but Polk Ridge. She loved her home, but the more she read, the more confined and imprisoned she felt in the small world of Polk Ridge. What lay beyond these beautiful mountains…

1958 Spangdahlem Air Force Base, Germany
Regina Ingram

At birth, Regina Marie Ingram managed to turn a structured and disciplined household upside down. Excited new parents Floyd and Louise had not anticipated the changes that a new baby would bring to their quiet base apartment.

They met during the Korean War when he served as a Staff Sargent in the Air Force and she as an enlisted nurse. The Korean War was the first independent combat for the United States Air Force, and Floyd was involved as air support on the ground in Korea. He enlisted as a member of the original U.S. Army Air Forces. Then came the Transfer Order 1 signed by President Harry S. Truman. This implemented and officially established the sector as the United States Air Force (USAF). He met Louise during his first few months in Korea, and for both of them, it was love at first sight. They married in December 1952 as soon as she completed her four years of service.

The regimented military life suited Louise, first as an enlisted nurse and then later as Floyd's wife. The birth of a baby, however, had been a more difficult transition. So far from home and family Gina (since Gina was much easier to coo and sing to a baby than Regina) had transformed a household from calculated and neat to chaotic and disarrayed. She would be the only addition.

Full of life and mischief, she was her father's child. A gregarious girl, she had her mom's blonde hair and blue eyes. She greeted each day with laughter and smiles. Most of those days were spent surrounded by the sights and sounds of military activity.

For overseas service families, everything they needed, from clothes to food, was available without ever leaving the base. From the groceries they bought at the commissary to the school Gina would attend in first grade, she never *needed* to go beyond the perimeter of the base. But Floyd and Louise *wanted* to see as much of the world as possible. So Gina's young life was spent exploring the beauty and history of many European countries.

Weekends found them visiting places in France, Belgium, Holland, and of course, Germany. They made sure she had a childhood filled with wonderful memories, sights, and sounds of different countries and different people.

Although she was too small to remember the actual visits, her mom made pictures of every place they took her. There were pictures when they visited the Eiffel Tower in Paris with its iron latticework towering far above the city streets. Pictures of the lunch they shared at the Altitude, a restaurant inside the tower. More pictures of a visit to the Louvre Museum, and its ancient art and artifacts from all over the world.

Snapshots of a young Gina filled several scrapbooks. Pictures in front of the Louvre Palace and Flanders Field Museum in Belgium. Photos of the Veldheer Tulip Garden in Holland with a little girl at center stage. There were even photos of a castle, Heidelberg Castle in Germany, with Gina entering through the gates. Every story of every visit had been retold to a young Gina so many times over that they became a permanent part of her memory.

By the time she reached Japan, she didn't need pictures to remember, but her mom continued to fill the scrapbooks anyway.

1968 Polk Ridge
Jorja Felsenthal

In many small rural towns, children from elementary school to high school attended class in one large building. In Polk Ridge, it was simply called Polk Ridge High School, and there were only 483 students the year Jo entered first grade. Going to school meant catching the bus with Stella. Somewhere around 7:15 (the exact time depended on the weather and the mood of Mr. Clancy, part-time bus driver, full-time farmer). Every morning, they walked to the end of the drive and waited for the big yellow bus. The bus would arrive in a swoosh of dust to whisk them way to a day filled with reading, writing, arithmetic…and recess!

Recess was her favorite part of the school day. As long as she had a book, recess opened the door to an imaginary world. Jo was more than eager to step in the pages and continue her journey across time and continents.

The year that Jo started fourth grade, Stella graduated, got married, and left. And although she had missed her sister's presence, her only comment had been that now she had to catch the bus by herself. Their daily lives were quite different. A much older Stella had no real interest in exploring or playing with a baby sister that often vexed her to the point of losing her temper. Jo, on the other hand, loved her outdoor adventures, and was quite oblivious to Stella's hostility.

Those years were spent roaming the surrounding woods, swimming in the creek that ran the length of the property, and reading.

She loved to read. As she read page after page, she discovered a world much larger than Polk Ridge. In fact, because of those books, she began to feel restless. Restless and ready to escape. When she opened a book she could escape. Visiting places across America, Europe, and Asia, anywhere in the world.

She imagined a visit to King Arthur's court, she became Scarlett O'Hara in Gone with the Wind, and even pretended to be Sinbad in The Arabian Nights.

The characters brought a new world to life for Jo. She poured through page after page. She read almost every book in the children's fiction section of the library. Time after time, she would hide in her closet late into the night, trying to finish the latest book that had captured her young mind; if not hiding in the closet, she was in the woods. It was this love of reading that most affected her as she grew older and she began to wonder what a life outside this small town would really be like.

"Daddy, you ever been anywhere but here?"

"You mean here in Polk Ridge, or somewhere other than Arkansas?"

"I mean, way away, you know, England or France?"

She'd just finished reading a book called "If I Were Going…" An old primer that had been donated to the public library. It told the story of other people in other countries.

"No, sweetheart, I've never been to those places. As a young man, I never had a hankering to go. I liked it here. By the time I gave any thought to seeing those places, I was married. A little too late to go. And besides, your momma and you and Stella are here. I don't need to go anywhere else."

"Well, I do. I need to see those places. I wanna see the people."

He laughed at his baby girl. Always needing to see it, to touch it, or talk about it.

"Well, Jo, when you grow up, why don't you go and see those places? Sometimes when we get older though, we change our mind. Lots of things change as we get older."

"Not me."

But all around her, life began to change, if not for Polk Ridge, for mainstream America. One of the first things she was able to remember would remain with her throughout life. A tragedy of such magnitude that even the young mind of a ten-year-old would remember: Martin Luther King was assassinated in Memphis, Tennessee. The upheaval and turmoil that came after didn't touch daily life in Polk Ridge; Relegated only to the television screen in the living room. As this occurred around her, as her days were spent worrying over her next chance to escape to the woods and read. Change did come, but it came slowly. Especially, to rural Ozark America, and many of those changes she continued to watch through scenes on a black and white screen.

The atmosphere of Haight-Ashbury and Woodstock never quite reached Polk Ridge. In a small town that boasted a population of less than 3000 during the 1950 census, the influence of LSD and hippies was hard to find.

Music, however, was a different story. Her mom loved music. Thanks to the Magnavox Stereo and record console that her dad had given her mom on their tenth anniversary, the house was often filled with music. Steel guitars and piano sounds accompanied the voices of Merle Haggard, Patsy Cline, Tammy Wynette, and Johnny Cash. Country music was a staple, but there were also the rockabilly sounds of Carl Perkins, Elvis Presley, and Jerry Lee Lewis. It was one of the first visible changes that crept into small town life during the late '60's.

The next signs of change would come with clothes, cars, and telephones. Skirts, trousers, and pedal pushers gave way to bell bottoms, halter tops, and platform shoes. Mustangs and Camaros replaced the Buicks and Chevys, and telephones made their way to Polk County. Thanks to cooperatives such as the National Rural Electric Cooperative Association, Polk County received a government loan and formed the Polk County Telephone Company.

Every rural farmer and family could have a telephone. Tom had a black rotary dial installed in the foyer, at the front entrance of the house. The infamous party line was born. A party line allowed one phone line to be shared between several families, and each family had a specific number assigned to them. Calls between families on the party line were made by simply dialing a three-digit number, holding down the switch hook, and waiting for the other phone to ring. Communication between families and friends no longer required an actual trip – you simply had to pick up the phone. The only catch: if you picked up the receiver during a conversation between two parties, you could listen, almost without detection. You could also tell if another party on your line was receiving a call because of the "humming" sound any of the phones on the line made when another rang. Communication was faster, and so was gossip.

Polk Ridge became smaller and smaller as she began to witness much of the change in the world around her. She continued to fill her mind with stories of other people and other places.

1968 Misawa Air Force Base, Japan
Regina Ingram

Life in Japan left Gina with two distinct memories: beautiful and meticulously manicured gardens, and the discovery of her dyslexia.

Military housing is military housing is military housing. It seemed to a young Gina that their new apartment looked eerily similar to their old apartment. Nothing changed from Germany to Japan when she looked around her room. The change she most remembered was in the area surrounding the new military base. She fell in love with Japanese gardens.

Exquisite in their colors, textures, and designs she experienced a new world of color. Orchids, Japanese maples, ponds filled with hundreds of colorful fish, Zen stones, raked sand, ornamental bridges, and tiny temples. She and her mom spent hours that first summer exploring the gardens and learning their history.

During first grade in Germany, Gina's teacher had approached Louise with the possibility that she might be dyslexic, and she recommended an evaluation to diagnose the condition. Louise had never heard of dyslexia, nor did she understand the symptoms; she did know and see the difficulty and frustration as Gina tried to learn her letters, and the anger and tears as she tried to read.

When they arrived at Misawa, Louise researched the symptoms of dyslexia. In her thoughts, her maternal mind began to accept the possibility.

Shortly after starting second grade, Mrs. Latham sent a note home with Gina requesting a conference, and Louise was certain that her intuition had been right. The doctor diagnosed Gina one month later with secondary visual dyslexia. He assured her that she would probably outgrow the condition but it would have an effect on her ability to read during elementary school.

That's when the tutoring began. Every day after school Gina spent an hour performing exercises. Balancing exercises, such as standing on one foot while her mom counted to ten or stepping over a stack of books with one eye closed. Then there were the visual skill exercises that required her to look at cue cards and memorize first pictures, and later letters. For Gina, the gardens became a means of escaping from the rigors of learning. She gazed upon their beauty and didn't have to memorize letters, read, or do exercises. Her thoughts free to imagine that she was a Japanese maiden, a French princess, or an English duchess, creating her own world among the beautiful gardens.

As they walked through the Sankeien gardens in Tokyo one Saturday morning, Gina was a usual chatterbox and pointed out varieties of plants and flowers that dotted the garden. She was so smart, so bright.

"Dad, sometimes I want to live in these gardens."

He looked down and noticed that her usually smiling and sunny face was creased and frowning.

"Why, baby?"

"Because I hate school. I try so very hard. But every day, I have to read, and do those hard exercises. It just doesn't come out right. It's always the same. The letters get all messed up, and I just can't put them together right."

It broke his heart to see his baby girl sad and frustrated. He and Louise had done everything they could to make her life as wonderful as possible, but this problem was beyond their control. She would have to conquer this on her own.. Some things simply had to be faced and conquered alone.

"Life will always be filled with hard things, Gina. It's how you handle the situation that makes your life good or bad. I understand that schoolwork is hard, but if you can stick with it, it will pass. You won't be in school forever, and the letters won't always be so messed up."

"Well, when I finish school, I'm never reading again. Then it won't matter if the letters are messed up. I can just look at the pictures, and somebody else can read," retorted Gina.

He smiled. So stubborn and determined. If the only thing she had to do was talk her way through life, she was going to be just fine.

During summer recess, the base organized camps for the elementary kids, which gave them the opportunity to interact with Japanese children. The scheduled visits included trips to the gardens, temples, and museums that surrounded the airbase. Gina loved Japanese culture and attended every summer camp, even learning to speak some of the language.

It was also in Japan that her dad introduced her to hiking, spending Saturday after Saturday exploring the Northern Alps of Japan.

He sensed that Louise needed a break from the constant strain of tutoring and sensory exercises and Gina needed time to relax as well. So on Saturday mornings, they headed to the mountains. She began to love hiking and the views from mountaintops as much as the gardens that surrounded her home. Breathtaking views from the tops of mountains that rose high above deep valleys. Valleys filled with crimson, yellow, and red. The sight made such an impression on the young girl that the mental images would be a part of her memory forever. Even as an adult, she only had to close her eyes to recall the vivid sights and sounds.

A visit atop a mountain, any mountain, never failed to remind her of her childhood and the wonderful Saturdays that she spent with her dad.

1970 Polk Ridge

Jorja Felsenthal

When Jo turned twelve, instead of just tagging along with her dad to the co-op, he offered her a summer job. And although she would have to give up her summer days roaming freely in the woods, she relished the paycheck she received on Fridays. The co-op was a joint venture of the Polk Ridge residents and farmers, a leftover organization from the Depression days. A time when it was often the only way to get seeds, fertilizers, fuel, and chemicals for crops. Tom had been hired on at the co-op right out of school as a helper. Thanks to years of hard work and devotion to customers, at thirty-nine he was now the general manager. Wiry and always moving, he never failed to lend a helping hand. His customers and fellow farmers developed a deep respect and fondness for him, something Jo would also come to respect.

The co-op was a mysterious and wonderfully chaotic place during the summer because of the increased visits and needs of residents and farmers alike. Crops had to be planted, and canning had to be done, and this usually meant a trip to the co-op for supplies.

Once you entered the gated yard you entered a maze of bags and crates. There were stacks and stacks of fertilizer in fifty-pound bags. Crates of seeds and plants that served as wonderful passages for her to walk through as she helped customers find a specific item. And there was, of course, the wonderland of complicated equipment that she never understood. She simply loved climbing on top and surveying the yard. Jo felt as though she had become the queen of the co-op!

Inside, the musty smell of old wood, diesel, grease and sweat greeted the nose. Cracked, hand-hewn planks creaked when customers and farmers walked across the floor, and dust covered everything in stock. Sometime halfway through the first summer of working, she understood why her dad loved his work. Not only was the co-op a wonderland of stuff, she always found a customer willing to talk. She, like her dad, truly enjoyed the farming families of the surrounding community. During that first summer, she heard more mountain legends, superstitions, and sayings than she could possibly remember. Her favorites came from Mr. Clancy.

Mr. Clancy--she was never sure if that was his first name or his last--had a new story or saying for her every time he visited the co-op.

He impressed young Jo with tales of the Indians that had once lived in the Ozark Mountains. There legend of the Great Fire Spirit of the Neosho Indians and Gideon Sims, the mountain man. When he exhausted those stories, he moved onto superstitions and old wives' tales. Tales such as "if you sneeze before breakfast, you'll have company before lunch," or "if your ears are burning, someone's talking about you." There were some that intrigued her more than others. She questioned him extensively over "if your left hand itches, you'll walk on strange ground". Had this ever happened to him? What kind of strange ground? Quite often there was a moral and lesson to be learned from each short saying. As each week of the summer passed, he imparted a new piece of valuable wisdom. Finally as it drew to a close, Mr. Clancy gave her some advice she would remember for the rest of her life. It came in the short sentences he imparted according to his perceived importance. *One, that which doesn't kill you will make you stronger. Second, nothing is impossible for the willing mind. And finally, don't cut off your nose to spite your face.*

He had to be the oldest farmer in Polk Ridge, and her favorite bus driver by far. He never wore anything but overalls, a John Deere cap, almost as old as he was, and farmers' lace-up boots. The front pocket of his overalls was stuffed with a pouch of the Levi Garrett tobacco he chewed, staining the stubble around his mouth. As though he didn't have time to spit. Everything about Mr. Clancy was weathered and worn, from his face to his overalls and his boots. He never failed to surprise Jo when he imparted some of the wisdom that lay hidden in the furrows of his mind.

She also would never forget the first time she saw him at the co-op.

He needed a replacement for the coulter (pronounced "cutter" by farmers) on his plow. The co-op had plows, shares, and beams – but no coulter.

"Weeell," he drawled in his mountain dialect, "I guess I'll jus' hav' to make one. I can't wait no two weeks for a spare. Gotta get that field plowed today or tomorr'at the latest. Ya gotta a table saw blade, or a circular saw blade? I believe I can fix it myself with one a' those."

At this, Jo looked at him with a curious stare. Make a cutter from a saw blade? She gave him a dubious look.

"Yes, sir, we got some twelve- and fourteen-inch blades, but I don't…"

"Girl, there's always more than one way to skin a cat," interrupted Mr. Clancy. "You gotta figure out a way when you ain't got much time, no money, and a livin' to make."

It took her several seconds to realize it wasn't a real cat he was speaking of. And, another ten to understand that sometimes you just gotta do what you gotta do, adapt and overcome. Something she would always remember.

The job at the co-op came with another benefit, other than an education in common sense and sayings, thanks to the fact that she *was* working for her dad. He had agreed if she had her work done, the stocking was complete, and there were no customers, she would be allowed to sit behind the counter and read. She kept the latest book stuffed under the checkout counter.

She took advantage of the opportunities before her to experience different people and different conversations whether in life or a book. The more she began to learn about the world around her, the more she wanted to learn. There was so much out there.

1970 Kunsan Air Force Base, South Korea
Regina Ingram

South Korea reminded Gina of Japan. There weren't any Japanese gardens in sight, but the mountains were familiar, and so were the struggles with reading and writing. It was sometime during her years in Korea that she decided if she could complete the twelfth grade, she would never look at another book. Never.

She also discovered her love of sports and cheerleading in Korea. Military life can take a toll on families, and especially the children of those families. When you move every four years or so, you grow accustomed to making and losing friends. At a time when most are beginning to widen their circle of friends, and have a "best" friend, Gina didn't have the chance. Sports and cheering made school more enjoyable, and anything that made school better she was willing to try.

School life on a military base isn't very different than any other school system. There are classes, cliques, sports, and rivalries with other base schools. Cheerleaders and football teams are as much a part of life on base schools as they are in small-town schools. There is, however, one major difference: children are constantly coming and going.

Unlike her friends, Gina seldom complained about constantly moving. It was a normal part of her life, and she enjoyed the change in cultures and locations. What she truly loved was cheering, and that was possible no matter where she lived.

She made friends easily and always had a story to tell involving some exotic place she'd been or a unique person she'd met. She was popular with her classmates, thanks to her love of chatter and being a petite, cute blond never hurt either.

As she made every effort to become a cheerleader, Gina and her dad also resumed their hikes, and she immersed herself in learning the Korean culture during their Saturday excursions.

It was on one of those hikes that Gina's conversation with her dad startled and worried him.

"Dad, we've been hiking for as long as I can remember, just you and me. But would you mind if we brought Alissa with us next time?"

"Now, which one is Alissa?"

"Oh, come on, Dad. Alissa. Long brown hair, skinny legs, and kind of loud?"

"Oh, yeah. No, I don't mind. You gettin' tired of me?"

"Nooo, I'm not getting tired of you, Dad. Never! But I've finally found somebody that has as much trouble at school as I do. I think I may finally have found a best friend, and I wanted to bring her with us. I want her to see why I love this so much. And, best friends are really hard to come by when you move every other year."

At that, he stopped in his tracks. He'd been so busy with his career, it had never occurred to him that his daughter was growing into a teenager, with the usual teenage hopes, dreams, and problems. It suddenly dawned on him that she had never experienced the kind of childhood he'd known. To grow up in one place, knowing the same people all your life, surrounded by family and lifelong friends. He and her mom had given her a lot when it came to experiences. However, the one experience he remembered so fondly in his own mind, that of his childhood home, she was going to miss.

She didn't realize that her dad had stopped, walking several feet before she turned to speak.

"What's wrong, Dad?"

"Nothing. I think a rock in my shoe. Give me a second and I'll catch up. And invite Alissa to join us. I would be honored to escort two beautiful young women on our next hike."

At this, she giggled and stopped to wait.

After a pile of paperwork and twenty-five years of service for his country, Floyd was ready to retire. It was time to give Gina a place that had roots, family, and *beautiful* mountains.

By 1972, Gina had lived on three different continents, in four different countries, and called six different airbases home. Now, it seemed time to finally give her a real home.

The Ingram family had called the Ozark Mountains home for many generations. Floyd's parents, Paulie and Adell still farmed and lived on their ancestor's land. Louise, having grown up in a large city, wasn't too excited when her husband wanted to return to Polk Ridge. The thought of staying with Miss Adell made her just a little bit uneasy. Her mother-in-law thought she lacked "useful skills", such as picking peas or canning, and they would be staying with them until Floyd could build a house. Her life had given her the opportunity to travel the world, to experience places filled with different cultures and languages. What would Polk Ridge have to offer? It certainly would not be quality time with her mother-in-law. And Polk Ridge was no Minneapolis, nor anything close to the airbases she had known.

Floyd, however, had made up his mind, and in the spring of 1972, he took his family home to Polk Ridge.

Gina knew the *world* around her but nothing of the Ozark Mountains in Arkansas.

CHAPTER 2

June, 1972
Jo & Gina

IT WAS A HOT summer in Polk Ridge when the two girls met.

Some would consider it fate--when you're in the right place at the right time. For them, simply perfect timing. The only thing Gina lacked, that she really wanted, was a best friend. The only thing Jo lacked, that she really wanted, was to meet someone to tell her about the world beyond Polk Ridge. Somehow, that summer, fate intervened and gave them exactly what they wanted.

Gina at once felt at home in Polk Ridge, and took to mountain life as though it were a calling, not merely a place to live. She had no trouble adjusting to her new community and was ready once again to explore everything that surrounded her.

Her dad had business at the co-op, and she decided to tag along. Once they returned to Polk Ridge, he bought some land and began the process of building a new house. He needed to make a trip to the co-op for lumber. Gina, tired of spending her days inside with her mom and Granny Adell, decided to tag along.

The co-op had evolved into more of a general store than a true co-op, and there were basic building materials right alongside animal feed and seed. As they pulled into the co-op's yard, Floyd told Gina to wait in the truck; he would only be a minute. But, as usual, she had other ideas, and in typical Gina fashion, persuaded her dad to let her wait inside.

She wanted to get out and get to know the folks of Polk Ridge, and the co-op seemed like a great place to start. Reluctantly, he agreed, and as she entered the co-op through the side door, he hailed Tom in the lumberyard.

It took her eyes a minute to adjust to the dim light of the interior, but once she could clearly see, she began to walk around. Dust covered everything, and there was a strong smell of sweet feed, fertilizer, and garden seeds that mingled together to create a scent she would never forget.

She made her way over to the only person working: Jo. Behind the counter, ringing up one of the farmers and fully immersed in her conversation she didn't notice Gina. Jo was chatting with him discussing the weather, the heat, and the lack of rain. Gina stood and watched as she finished her sale, and went over to introduce herself.

"Hi, I'm Gina Ingram, and my dad, mom, and I have recently moved here. My dad's outside looking at some lumber, and I was wondering…could you tell me where I might find some rope and a cage?"

"Oh, yeah. My daddy told me about y'all moving back here. You're stayin' over at the Ingram home place with Mr. Paulie and Miss Adell. I'm Jorja, or rather Jo as everyone around here calls me. My dad runs the co-op an' I help him during the summer.

"We've got some rope right back here, and what kinda cage are you looking for? Is it for a dog or a cat?" She studied Gina and determined they seemed to be the same age, but she quickly realized that Gina wasn't from anywhere close to Polk County, or Arkansas for that matter; her enunciation gave her away.

"No, it's for catching a bird – my dad told me he would take me snipe hunting. I wanted to have a rope and cage to put it in."

Jo burst into laughter.

"I hate to disappoint you, but there's no such thing as a snipe, Gina. It's just a joke that's been handed down from generation to generation, something for fun. Your daddy will take you out into the woods and show you how to set up a cage to catch a bird. Next, he'll pretend that he's gonna go scare one up and he'll leave you there for a couple of hours or longer. You'll be waitin' for somethin' that never arrives."

She watched as Gina's expression changed from one of complete disbelief, to one of mischief.

"Well," she confided, "you don't mention that you explained that to me while we were talking. I believe I'll have some fun of my own with my dad."

Thirty minutes later, Floyd came inside the co-op to get Gina, only to find the two girls immersed in conversation and laughter. This was only the beginning.

That summer, the girls began the closest friendship they had ever known. During the early days, their different personalities drew them together. The more they talked and spent time together, the more they exchanged information and ideas. Gina loved listening to Jo talk. Her voice, soft with the cadence of the Ozark dialect and slang, mesmerized Gina, and contrasted sharply to Gina's clipped accent.

Jo, on the other hand, always begged for more stories from Gina.

"Please tell me about South Korea again. I wanna hear about the towns and the gardens there. Did they have lots of woods or forests? You've already told me about school and the people, but what about the towns--do they have mountains there, too?"

"Goodness, yes. My dad loves the mountains, and since he was so far from his home here, he would take us out on Saturdays to explore the mountains there. Let me think, there was Namsan, Gasan, Buramsan, Jangsan and Gajisan, and we visited them several times.

Lots of 'sans', huh? Namsan was my favorite. It's right outside of Seoul and so beautiful in the fall. They have a park, a beacon tower, a cable car, and you can see the skyline of Seoul from on top. One time we had to wait 'til late in the afternoon to hike, so it was almost dark by the time we got to the top. The lights in Seoul began to twinkle when we got there. It was so cool. I always wanted to race to the top, mostly to explore and poke around, but that time was truly beautiful. Their trees are different but still just as green, and their flowers are all kinds of colors, just the same as here. In the fall, there are reds, yellows, oranges everywhere, it resembles a patchwork quilt."

"I wish I could go and see the people there. I read this stuff all the time, but that's just it. I only get to read. I want to go there."

"Yes, but it's just as beautiful here, Jo. You just don't have a bunch of people talking in a language you don't understand, or…" Gina giggled. "Sometimes you do. I sure am having a hard time with some of the words y'all use." She tried mimicking Jo's Ozark drawl.

This conversation, and many others, usually took place at the Dairy Queen or the woods, places where they would sit and talk for hours.

Gina had a million questions concerning the upcoming school year. What kind of clothes were Jo going to get to go back to school? How many girls were going to be in their class? Did she like any boys? Did she know most of the teachers? Did they have football? Did they have any sports for girls?

"Well, there are usually twelve girls, not including me, and fourteen boys. You've already met Shelly, Melissa, and Gloria, We saw them last week here at the Dairy Queen. And you met Paul. You'll at least know five of us. Yes, we have football, only volleyball for girls, and cheerleading. And no, I don't have a boyfriend. I don't want one. I'd rather read."

"Read? Not me. I hate books. I hate studying, and I hate reading.

I want to be a cheerleader." She smiled as she threw her hands up to form a V and crossed one leg over the other. "See, I'm a natural!"

"I'd rather spend my afternoon at the co-op working or studying than cheerleader practice. You can have it."

Jo was exhausted from answering so many questions and finally asked Gina if she wanted to go shopping with her to get their clothes for school. "That way, you'll know what to wear," she said. "You may not know anybody or any teachers, but at least you'll have some great clothes."

Looking good didn't seem too hard for Gina. She was petite, to say the least, and weighed only seventy-five pounds that summer. Jo, on the other hand was taller-- still slender, but not nearly as graceful as Gina.

Oh, well, that's the difference between the city mouse and the country mouse. Another one of those "sayings" from Mr. Clancy.

As Gina's dad worked to finish their new home, she worked as hard at having a great time with her new friend. Since Jo spent her mornings at the co-op, they only had the afternoons to hang out, but they made the best of those afternoons. Swimming, riding bikes, ice cream at the Dairy Queen, and creating adventures that only young girls invent while roaming around a small mountain community. They both loved the mountains and disappeared afternoons on their bikes, investigating hiking trails and new swimming holes. Maureen and Louise had a difficult time keeping track of their daughters, and Maureen often had to assure Louise that they would return from their rambling adventures in one piece.

On one particular sunny mountain afternoon, as the girls made their way to the Dairy Queen for their mid-afternoon ice cream rendezvous, Gina stopped her bike abruptly. There, some hundred yards or so in front of them she saw a huge black object in the road.

The black object detected their presence at the same time Gina brought her bike to a screeching halt. The bear raised himself to full height as he stood on his back legs and surveyed them. He was the tallest, scariest animal she had ever seen.

Black bears are native to the Ozarks. They were near extinction in the '30s and '40s, but by the time the girls travelled the roads around Polk Ridge, they once again numbered in the hundreds. This bear had apparently made Polk Ridge its home, right alongside the townspeople and Jo was fully accustomed to the haphazard appearance of "Bear" on the side of the road. Although she knew that bears were dangerous, this Bear was a different story. She calmly halted her bike as well.

"Jo," Gina whispered. "What are we going to do?"

"Gina," she whispered back in a mocking whisper, "we're gonna do what we always do."

"Well," she said, in a tone growing more desperate with each passing second, "what exactly is that?"

"We're gonna ask him if he needs a ride," Jo giggled as she turned to study Gina.

Her face had become a mixture of stark fear, disbelief at her friend's remark, and the stance of a caged animal, searching for a way to escape.

"Bear's always lurkin' somewhere around here. We see him all the time. He won't bother you; he's only lookin' for food. He wanders around town sometimes when he's got a hankerin' for something sweet. He loves the doughnuts from Dairy Queen. Since we're goin' there, we'll pick him up a few and drop them off later. Right now, we'll simply go the other way around.

Gina's facial expression didn't change as Jo explained how Bear came to be the "town bear". She certainly had doubts when it came to picking up doughnuts to feed to him.

"I'm *not* coming back by and bringing him *anything*. He might decide he'd rather eat us than the doughnuts," she declared as she turned her bike around to follow Jo and take the other way around.

Jo, taking immense pleasure in Gina's evident fear, simply laughed as she hopped back on her bike and pedaled into town. She already realized fate had dropped a lifelong friend into her lap. And from what she could tell, Gina did too.

Freshman Year, 1972

True to her word, Jo asked her mom if they could go school shopping with Gina and her mom. Maureen reluctantly agreed. Explaining during the conversation with her daughter that she hardly knew Louise. She wasn't sure Louise wanted to go over to Little Rock just to buy school clothes.

"I realize your daddy has spoiled you rotten by lettin' you go every year all the way over there just to get clothes, but everybody might not wanna do that."

"Please, Momma, just call Miss Louise and ask if they wanna go. I promised Gina I would take her with us. She's new, and she doesn't have any other friends to go shoppin' with. Just *please* ask."

And so, on the third day of August, the four of them set out for Little Rock in the bright red Chevy Chevelle that Gina's dad bought for Louise. He had given it as a gift to appease her for moving her to such a small town and having to stay with Miss Adell.

It was hot, and Little Rock was a seventy-five-mile trip one way. The car wasn't air-conditioned, and there were four females stuck in one car--all the makings of a long, long, trip.

While the girls chatted in the back, Maureen and Louise made small talk. Maureen had worried after talking to Louise on the phone that they would have little in common. From everything she had heard, Louise came from a big city and had travelled a lot during their time in the military. She wasn't accustomed to small-town life and Maureen wondered what *she* could possibly say that would interest Louise.

Louise, on the other hand, gave it her best effort. She needed to make at least a few friends if she was going to spend the rest of her life in Polk Ridge. Maureen was, so far, the first to invite her to do anything, and shopping was something she enjoyed. Surely, she could succeed at shopping and making a new friend, even in this God-forsaken place.

Not very long into the trip, they discovered they did have one thing in common: their husbands truly enjoyed spoiling their daughters. The rest of the trip was spent discussing the hardships of raising daughters, dealing with the fathers of those daughters, and trying to start a friendship of their own.

Maureen had spent her entire life raising kids and tending gardens. She had never been to Germany, Japan, Korea, or any of the other places Louise had visited. But she did know about having a husband and hard work. It seemed that Louise understood something about those two things as well.

Generally, husbands got what they wanted, and the hard work at home was borne by the wife.

The girls paid little attention to their mothers' conversation. They were too busy trying to determine what to buy with the money they had been given to accomplish their "wardrobe" mission.

The four of them arrived in Little Rock around 10 a.m., and by 2 p.m., the girls had several bags of clothes in tow.

Jo saved the best place for last though. These final purchases were going to be a tough sell to her momma, and Miss Louise. She wanted to make sure they were near exhaustion before she asked to go.

She made Gina ask.

"Mom," Gina began, "can we go to the new University Mall?

There's a Dillard's there, and Shelly told us last week at the co-op that they've got some cool new clothes. I've never been to Dillard's, and they've got an escalator!"

Now, Jo's turn.

"An escalator? You ever rode on one of those? I haven't. Momma, you ever been on an escalator?"

"No, Jo. I've never been on an escalator, but you girls should have enough clothes by now. How much money do you have left?"

"Almost fifty dollars. I only need one or two more tops, and a new pair of shoes."

"Gina," Louise chimed in, "what about you? Spent dry?"

"No. I still have sixty dollars," replied Gina.

"You guys can sit outside Dillard's in the mall and have some ice cream while we finish our shopping," Jo suggested.

"Fine," Maureen agreed. "But don't you get in there and buy some outlandish outfit your daddy won't let you wear."

"Yes, ma'am," she chimed, with her fingers crossed. They already knew what they were looking for, and Dillard's had it.

When they finished in Dillard's, each girl had a new mini-skirt. One bright blue and one bright green. Platform shoes with psyche-delic soles and matching tie-dyed halter ruffle tops.

As they left the store, they spotted their mothers sitting beside the Baskin Robbins, eating ice cream cones.

"Listen, Gina, just show them the shoes. They'll be so wrapped up in that that maybe they won't ask to see the rest."

Jo was well aware of what she was doing. Sure enough, they never got past the psychedelic soles. There were no questions about the rest of the items in the bag; at least not until they were halfway home, and by then it was too late.

The next day, Floyd entered the co-op in search of a new shovel and Tom. As he approached his friend, he noticed the slight scowl, and worried crease on his brow.

"Are you okay?" Floyd asked.

"Did you by chance talk to your daughter after their shopping trip yesterday?"

"Yep. You lost too, uh…?"

"Yep." And with that, Tom moved on.

"So what can I help you find today?" he asked.

Both men understood, in less than twenty words, that their daughters were growing up; clothes were just the beginning.

"Oh, well," Floyd mused. "At least they got what they wanted."

"Yeah, and to quote Jo, 'they'll look really cool,'" Tom mimicked in his daughter's young voice.

Gina woke up early the first day of school and carried more than a few butterflies in her stomach. She was nervous—really nervous.

They decided to wear the Dillard's outfit on the first day of school. But even Gina, who was accustomed to different kinds of people and clothes, remained a little doubtful. It might be a bit too much; the skirt *was* very short.

Oh well. *I'm not going to impress the teachers as much as my classmates,* thought Gina. I'll never be an A student, so I might as well be the social butterfly. This is my chance to make an impression. Snazzy clothes can only help. If I'm going to get to spend the rest of high school here, I want to make as many friends as I can.

She surveyed herself in the mirror as she dressed and prepared herself for her father's stern look at the breakfast table.

On the other side of Polk Ridge, Jo was having a few second thoughts herself. She had already faced her daddy once with the outfit on when they'd returned from Little Rock. She really didn't want to see the scowl again this morning. *Maybe he's already gone to work,* she thought.

She made her way downstairs to the kitchen where her momma and breakfast waited.

"Well, Jo, you dressed nice this morning. I've fixed you egg, toast, and grits. Are you ready for high school?" The thought of her last girl entering high school created a sadness for her that morning. She didn't want an argument or tension. She just wanted to remember this day with happiness.

"Yes, Momma. Where's Daddy? Already gone to work?"

"Yeah, you know he's having a little trouble adjusting to all this change. It's bad enough that his baby girl is growing up, but now he's gotta watch the things he's accustomed to change as well. The clothes, the hair, and even the music. It's just hard for him."

Jo thought what it must be like for him. Most of her thoughts were always about her, not her parents. She'd never contemplated the fact that her daddy might not be in such a hurry for her to grow up.

"I'm sorry it's so hard for him, and I guess you, too. I just wanna be like everybody else, Momma. I just wanna fit in."

With that, she sat down to eat her breakfast and wait on Gina and her mom. They were coming by to pick her up, so she didn't have to take the bus on the first day.

A week before school started, Louise registered Gina for classes, making sure that she had everything she needed for the first day. She got a copy of her daughter's class schedule as well. The doctors in Japan and Korea had assured Louise that Gina would outgrow dyslexia, but she still had difficulty with reading. Deep inside, she worried. She didn't want her daughter to start high school with reading problems. It seemed as though it wasn't going away though, not just yet. Louise went to the office and scheduled conferences with Gina's teachers as the girls went straight to the ninth grade homeroom.

The ninth grade homeroom was in the Ag and Home Economics building and was adjacent to the main school. The girls arrived early, and there were only two other people in the room: Paul Collections and Robert Phillips.

"Hey, Paul. Hey, Robert. You both got here early, I see. Paul, your daddy drop you off on the way to work, and Robert, I bet your uncle did on his way to the mill, right?"

Paul spoke first. "Hi, Jo. Yeah, you know he's gotta get to work early, which means I get to school early. Hi, Gina, you girls look nice today. Where'd ya get those outfits?"

"Little Rock. We went shopping with my mom and Miss Maureen. Thanks. You don't look too shabby yourself."

Robert just stared at Gina. They hadn't met until now. Finally he spoke.

"Jo, you wanna introduce me?"

"Oh, sure. I forgot that you guys haven't met. Gina Ingram, this is Robert Phillips. His uncle and daddy work over at the sawmill on the way to Flowood, on Highway 388."

"Hi, nice to meet you," said Gina.

At that, Shelly and Gloria came in the room and captured the girls' attention. Robert's attention, however, was still on Gina.

Paul was a little on the quiet side--not athletic, although his build would have led you to believe he was. His dad owned the local winery, and he spent much of his free time working and learning the ins and outs of growing and making of some of Arkansas' "finest wine." At least that's what his daddy always said, so he made sure to repeat it whenever asked. His face was still very boyish, with brown hair and brown eyes. More handsome than cute, he was having a hard time growing into a young man. In addition to his boyish appearance, his voice was also changing and he would go from a normal sound to a high-pitched squeak, right in mid-sentence. This often brought a crimson blush to his face, and so, for now, he tried not to talk unless it was necessary.

Robert, on the other hand, was already taller than Paul, handsome and athletic. He was the oldest of ten children and spent most of his time either on a football or baseball field. Like Jo, he was looking for a way out of Polk Ridge, and athletics would have to be the ticket. There just wasn't a lot of money to spare in the Phillips household for college.

Homeroom filled up with more students, and Jo introduced Gina to everyone as they came through the door. Mrs. Bryant, the homeroom teacher, who was now seated at the front of the classroom, had frowned slightly as she watched the girls greet their classmates.

"Jo, would you come up here just a second?" asked Mrs. Bryant.

She walked slowly to the front of the room. Dreading the question that she was going to be asked.

"Don't you think that skirt's just a little bit too short for school? Did your daddy see you this morning?"

"No, ma'am, I don't, and he didn't. But he saw it the other day. Momma said it looked very cool though."

"Well, you're here to learn, not 'look cool.' Just remember that. I hope you're going to be a good influence on our new student, right?"

At that moment, the 7:50 a.m. bell rang. Mrs. Bryant got her class's attention and called roll. At fifty-eight, she was a veteran in the classroom and knew the drill, almost to perfection. As soon as she finished accounting for her twenty-seven students, she called Gina to the front of the class.

"Gina," said Mrs. Bryant, "I'd like you to introduce yourself to your new classmates and tell us a little something about yourself. We're glad to have you at Polk Ridge High School, and I look forward to getting to know you as well."

Gina wasn't prepared for this. She had never had a teacher who asked new students to introduce themselves.

Oh my gosh, what am I gonna say? I never even met most of these people until today. What do I tell them? Where am I from? Germany, Japan, Korea… I guess I could just pick one…

All these thoughts swirled through her head as she made her way to the front of the class.

"Hi, everyone," she began a little falteringly. "My name is Gina Ingram, and I've just moved here from South Korea. My dad is retired from the military, and since he grew up here, he wanted to move back. I truly like it here, so far, and the mountains…."

Much to her relief, the bell rang before she could finish her sentence. Mrs. Bryant, giving them instructions to proceed to their first class, was drowned out by the sudden activity. Voices and rushing bodies of freshmen students in a hurry to get to first period. A new chapter in a new book had just begun: the story of Jo and Gina.

Polk Ridge High School Freshman Class, 1972

Shelley Atwater	*Pam Meadows*
Janet Barnett	*Tim McHenry*
Paul Collections	*Harry Noble*
Patsey Cooper	*Robert Phillips*
Lisa Davidson	*Melissa Pittman*
Terry Donavon	*Grace Plyler*
Jorja Felsenthal	*Keith Robertson*
Bill Forrest	*Beth Rimes*
Bobby Hays	*Judy Rogers*
Regina Ingram	*Melinda Riley*
Mary Ann Johnson	*Lloyd Simms*
Gloria Jones	*Joe Toms*
Todd Killen	*Donna Tucker*
Sammy Lavern	*David Williams*
Frank Madison	*Corbin Wilson*

March, 1973

1972-73 was a banner year for the Polk Ridge Yellow Jackets. Football and basketball seasons brought winning titles and trophies home to be displayed in the glass case that commanded much of the space in the hall of the high school. The case sat just as you entered the front doors, filled with trophies of accomplished teams.

Schoolwork consumed Jo's free time, but her best friend and reading were close seconds. She was already working on the valedictorian's spot, and nothing came between her A's and homework—not even Gina.

Gina's social education at Polk Ridge was doing much better than her academic one, but her mom continued to offer encouragement. She was never going to enjoy learning, but as the year progressed, an amazing thing began to happen. Call it luck, or call it the magic of friendship, the letters finally began to make sense for Gina.

The girls spent hours together studying and somewhere along the way, reading became easier for Gina. Grades got better, and eventually B's and C's became A's and B's.

Now, her report cards were dotted with A's and B's and she didn't dread bringing them home. Too bad socializing wasn't also a grade; that would have put her at the top of the class.

The winter of '72-'73 was reluctant to turn into spring that year. Snow still covered the ground when Gina saw the flyer posted on the bulletin board in the school hallway.

CHEERLEADER TRYOUTS, MARCH 13TH

Grades 6 – 8 Junior High 6 Positions
Grades 9 - 11 Senior High 10 Positions

See Mrs. Cobb, Cheerleader Sponsor for Application
Practice will begin March 3rd

That was exactly what she needed to see. She made her way to second period with her head in the clouds. She was going to participate in cheerleader tryouts.

Finally, something I really, really want to do, Gina thought.

Study hall followed their second-period class, and she was bursting with excitement.

"Jo," she began in her most persuading and cajoling tone, "let's try out for the cheerleading team on the 13th. It'll be fun, and you won't be working *the entire* day during the summer. You would have time for practice."

Jo simply glared. "Seriously? You *want* to spend your summer days sweating, screaming, and practicing just to *cheer* at a ballgame?"

She had no trouble thinking of at least fifty better ways to spend her summer afternoons. And besides, she was as athletic as the bear they had encountered last summer. Even now, she was still taller than Gina by a good six inches, and although she was quite slender, she was not cheerleader material. She had no trouble hiking and swimming. But twirling, tumbling and rhythm were not her strong suits.

"No, I'm not the slightest bit interested in *cheering*," she replied, in a tone that was almost a sneer, and left little doubt concerning her position.

Gina tried one more time.

"But we would have a ball, and it's so cool to be a cheerleader."

"Listen, I'm all about bein' *'cool'*, but I'm not about to spend all my time jumpin' around like a jack-in-the-box, sweaty and hot, when I could be reading or hiking. Or for that matter, workin' at the co-op. NO."

CHAPTER 3

1975

VIETNAM IS OVER, AND some 30,000 young men migrate to Canada to avoid the draft. Hundreds of thousands more protest America's involvement.

The United States is in the throes of a recession; unemployment is over 9 percent.

The national average for a gallon of gas is 44 cents.

Jimmy Hoffa disappears.

The Personal Computer is invented and offered for sale as a "build-it-yourself kit" by a company known as MITS.

The Rolling Stones, Queen, ZZ Top, Bad Company, and Aerosmith dominate the music scene.

It's senior year for Jo and Gina. Their whole life is in front of them.

Summer 1975

Summer of '75 brought with it opportunity, reward, and revelation, in just that order.

Gina wanted to work that summer. She approached her mom and dad before school ended. Although it might be hard for her to find a job, she still wanted one nonetheless. She'd watched Jo work for the last couple of summers and saw the satisfaction on her face when she deposited her check every week at the bank in Polk Ridge. Gina decided it was time to give it a try as well. She just wasn't sure where or how. Fitting a job into her practice schedule wasn't going to be easy, but her parents had agreed that it might be a good idea. Her mom even offered to drive her to work as well as practice. However, she would have to pay for gas when Louise drove her to work, and she would have to find the job on her own.

It finally fell into place during the conversation she had with Jo at the Dairy Queen. It was that conversation that actually landed her a job. They had stopped by their first day out of school for milkshakes to discuss work possibilities. There just weren't that many places for a teenage girl to work. As they sat down and started their list of possibilities, Melvin came by their table.

Melvin Kroon was the manager at the Dairy Queen, and like Gina, he wasn't from Polk Ridge.

He had moved there in May from Mobile, Alabama. Dairy Queen had transferred him from a store in Mobile where he had been working as an assistant manager. But this was his store. His first to manage on his own. At twenty-two, he was the product of a new management training program Dairy Queen had implemented. He was also one of the youngest they had ever promoted to title of manager. He'd gotten the location in Polk Ridge in part because it was a small town, and even as young as he was, could be handled by an inexperienced manager. The other reason was simply money. This particular location wasn't one of the most productive, and Melvin could live with the salary it would provide. Especially if it was a stepping stone to something better.

"Jo, I'm not sure where to start, because I have to be at practice by 9, Monday through Wednesday, and by 7 on Thursday. That only leaves afternoons and Friday. Who's gonna hire somebody that tells them when they can work?"

"Hey, girls. Milkshakes again today?" asked Melvin.

"Yup, we gotta find Gina a job, and milkshakes help us sort it out. She wants to make some money this summer, and it's gonna be pretty hard to find somebody to hire her."

At that moment, Melvin had an epiphany. He wasn't the most seasoned manager, but he did grasp one thing: Gina would be a great waitress and carhop, especially on Friday and Saturday afternoon. She was petite, blonde, and loved to talk.

"Well, we always hire extra summer help here, and I've only filled one of the spots. I've got another one open. There's only one catch: will your folks let you work on Sunday? Not every Sunday since we rotate between the regulars and summer part-time help. But it pays okay, and you get to keep your tips. What do ya say? Wanna try it out?"

It was just that simple. She started the following Friday, working the 1 to 8 shift in the afternoon. Still plenty of time left at 8 to cruise around town and socialize.

Two weeks passed by, and Gina picked up the phone to call Jo one morning. It was 8 a.m. on a Monday morning and practice started at 9, but she just had to tell Jo what she got for her birthday. It wasn't supposed to arrive until Friday, but the dealership brought it out as soon as it arrived, and she was dying to show Jo.

Please let her be at work already, thought Gina. I can swing by on my way to practice. It won't be nearly as far as her house… oh, pick up, pick up…

"Polk Ridge co-op, can I help you?" asked Jo.

"You won't believe what I got for my birthday, it's—"

Jo interrupted, "It's not your birthday yet. Not until Friday."

"That's right, it's not until Friday, but I got my present today. Are you gonna be at the co-op for the next thirty minutes? I'm gonna come by if you are." (Sometime over the last three years, Gina had picked up the slang and dialect of the Ozarks natives.)

Both girls heard the click on the line in between their sentence.

"Granny Adell, is that you?" Gina asked. There was a moment of silence. "Granny?" she asked somewhat louder this time.

"Yeah, are you on the phone, 'Gina?" (She never managed to call Gina by her full name.) "I wanted to call the co-op to see if those seeds I ordered last week were in. I can wait 'til y'all get finished."

"That's okay, Miss Adell. This is Jo, at the co-op. I'm here at work, and yes, your seeds came in yesterday."

"Well, thank you, sweetheart. I'll see if Floyd can drive me over this afternoon." With that, they were pretty sure Granny Adell had hung up the phone.

"My God, this phone system is ridiculous," said Gina. "You never know who's listenin'. My granny knew I was on the phone—she just wanted to hear what I was sayin'. I think she just sits beside the phone, waiting for it to hum."

"Yeah, so does my granny. They're afraid they might miss some good gossip." Jo couldn't help but laugh. Those old women needed something to do, and gossiping was it.

"Well, anyway. I'm gonna be here. You'll have to hunt me up when you get here. I may be in the back of the store."

"No, meet me out front in twenty minutes. I gotta get to practice. 'Bye."

She hung up before she could give Jo time to ask what the present was.

Twenty minutes later, Gina pulled into the yard at the co-op. Jo stood there, mouth gaping.

Gina waved the minute she turned off the highway, laughing and squealing at the same time. She was driving a brand new 1976 red Mustang convertible.

"Good Lord, how'd you get that? You realize how much them things cost? It's beautiful, but oh my gosh, how fast does it go?" She spewed questions faster than Gina could answer.

"I don't know how fast it will go, yet. The speedometer says 120. Ain't it beautiful? I never expected somethin' like this. Everybody's gonna want to ride with us!"

They spent the next ten minutes gushing over the car and making plans for Friday night.

"I gotta go. I'm gonna be late for practice, and it's never good when the head cheerleader is late. I don't have to work this afternoon, so you want me to come over after lunch?"

"Heck yeah, I want you to come over! I wanna go for a ride. I'll be finished at 1 p.m. Come by and get me, and we'll go by the house so I can change."

At that, Gina sped off to practice, basking in the glow of the best birthday present she'd ever gotten and appearing downright giddy behind the wheel.

Friday is gonna be fantastic, thought Gina. I don't have to work, got a date with Robert, and Jo and Paul are going on their first date! And we get to do it in my brand new Mustang! Ahhhh… life is great!

Throughout the warm sunny days of 1975, the girls went about their usual summer routine. Jo spent her mornings at the co-op while Gina practiced and worked a few afternoons a week at the Dairy Queen.

She had, in fact, taken the Dairy Queen by storm and somehow earned the nickname "Queenie," thanks to Melvin. Only twenty-two and not yet married, he found himself quite smitten with Gina. She never noticed nor gave him the time of day during that short summer—she was too busy falling in love with Robert.

While Robert and Gina were moving at the speed of light in their relationship, Jo and Paul seemed stalled. Their relationship moved at a much slower and much rockier pace, making little progress as the summer sailed by.

As much as they had in common, it was difficult for them to make small talk. Paul had so much he wanted to say; it just wasn't swimming, or hiking, or reading, or for that matter, his work. It was about his feelings, and there really never seemed to be a chance to say what was on his mind. Jo took his lack of conversation as lack of interest, and would've probably called it quits after the third date had it not been for Robert.

It was at the co-op one July morning that Robert managed to save Paul from certain dismissal. When he stopped by to pick up some guano to fertilize the garden, Jo composed her thoughts and asked Robert his opinion.

"I don't think Paul cares for me that much. He doesn't talk much, and he's not even tried to kiss me yet. What do you think?"

"Jo, just give him a little time. I think he really likes you. Not everybody talks non-stop. Some people, especially guys, just don't have a lot to say. You two make it hard for us to get a word in at all lots of times."

"No, we don't. You get to talk just as much as we do. You just don't wanna talk about clothes, or fashion, or what's goin on in the world. It's all football or baseball, or whatever."

"Just have a little patience and don't be so bossy when we're on a date. You need to chill out and let him decide a thing or two."

"Yeah, well, that might take longer than we've got on a date. He don't ever get in a hurry to make a decision."

"Yes, he does. You just get in too much of a hurry. And he's probably scared to death to try to kiss you since you never shut up and never let him decide anything on a date. Maybe he's waitin' on you to tell him when to kiss you." At that Robert flashed her a grin.

"Whatever. We'll see this Friday night. I won't decide anything. I'll be quiet when it's time to pick somethin'."

"Sure you will. Right after pigs fly," Robert laughed. "See ya Friday night."

Their Friday night began as usual for the four of them. Gina and Robert first went by to pick up Jo, and then out to the Collections' home to pick up Paul. Gina was still infatuated with her new car, so date night would once again be in the Mustang. First stop, the Dairy Queen for something to eat, next, on to cruise Main Street, and socialize with the other kids in town. Finally, sometime around 9, they found themselves out at the Old Iron Bridge.

Gina let the top down on the Mustang while they were in town. The drive out to the bridge was filled with the sounds of The Captain & Tennille's "Love Will Keep Us Together," and the humid air of a southern summer night.

"C'mon, Gina, let's go for a walk," said Robert.

"Walk? I don't wanna go for a walk. Let's stay here and listen to the music. Some of the others will be out here in a little bit, and we can get out and talk."

"I've got something I wanna show you over by the bridge sign. I saw it the other day, and I want you to see it—you don't even have to read the sign."

"Haha, that's soooo funny," she replied with sarcasm.

"I'll go, Robert. She can stay here with Jo," offered Paul.

"No, I want her to go. C'mon, let's go."

All four piled out of the car. Robert and Gina to go "see" what it was Robert had found, and Jo and Paul to lean against the back of the car and talk.

The warm breeze caught Jo's auburn hair, blowing it across her face. At that moment, Paul made up his mind to step closer, close his eyes, and hope for the best.

Instead of a soft kiss, he became entrapped in soft strands of hair. Jo giggled.

"Paul, if you wanna kiss me, give me a heads up, and I'll make sure you don't get a mouthful of hair."

His face was bright crimson.

"Well, can I kiss you?"

"Yes, you most certainly can. Right now would be a good time."

He's so nervous. No wonder he hasn't tried to kiss me; his face is red as a beet.

Jo grabbed her errant hair and moved closer.

This time, he tasted the warm, sweet softness of her lips, and his arms encircled her waist. Passion sprang to life inside them, spilling over and intensifying with each kiss.

Oh my…

In what seemed like only a very short time, but was in reality some thirty minutes, Robert and Gina returned from their sightseeing adventure. Paul and Jo never noticed, not until Robert cleared his throat.

"Mmm, sorry to interrupt you two, but I see headlights, and I thought you might want to join Gina and me in the car."

Robert's grin was unmistakable, even in the dim light of the summer moon. He gave Jo an *I-told-you-so* look and hopped in the driver's seat.

Friday nights at the Old Bridge took on a new meaning for Jo and Paul.

As July came to a close, the girls got ready to make their usual trip to Little Rock. They only had a couple of weeks left before school started, and a trip of this magnitude, required careful planning.

They spent the afternoon of the first Friday of August at their favorite swimming hole laying out their plans.

By four o'clock, they were on their way home. The afternoon at the old iron bridge had been spent swimming and planning their trip. They were hot, wet, and sun-drenched. As they pulled in Gina's drive, Jo noticed her dad's truck.

That's weird.. I don't think I'm in trouble.

"Hey, reckon why my dad's here?"

"I don't have a clue, we ain't done anything, I don't suppose. C'mon, let's go see."

As they entered through the front door, they saw their dads sitting at the kitchen table.

"What are you doing here, Dad? It's not time for the co-op to close. Is everything alright?" Jo asked, with more than a little apprehension. She didn't think she was in trouble. At least, she couldn't remember anything she'd done that would warrant a "meeting of the fathers."

"We both wanted to talk to you girls, and no, you're not in trouble; I can see that look on your face. We just want to talk to you about an opportunity."

Unknown to the girls, the two men had visited several weeks earlier, to discuss this "opportunity" that Floyd earnestly wanted to investigate.. Something that would be a life changing event for the girls. Something that, until 1975, had never been an option for a woman.

The United States military, since World War II, had been the most powerful military force in the world. Nothing surrounding their prowess was changing. Their ranks, however, were. Currently, the only cadets graduating from military academies were men.

During the early months of the year, he had followed closely legislation that was going to make history. Women's rights groups and the feminist movement had pushed legislation that would allow female cadets in every branch of the military. It was scheduled for a vote in September, and President Ford had given his nod of approval. If passed, he would sign it.

He recognized what a chance the girls had. If he helped to get them in, they would be the first class of female cadets to graduate. Opportunity would be theirs if they wanted it.

He'd gone by the co-op as soon as he was certain the legislation was going to pass, sat down with Tom and laid out his plan. It would be hard--not only to get them in, but for them to make it as the first class of female cadets. There would be prejudice, and rigorous requirements. But, as he pointed out, times were changing. He believed they deserved more than a life in Polk Ridge would afford. He, more so than Tom, understood that the military could provide them with an education and a chance at a career. It was with pride that he included the fact that their daughters would be making history. Military history as well as American history.

Tom had already graduated one daughter and handed her off in marriage to a man that, although he was a wonderful husband and father, had very little ambition. His eldest daughter's life had not been what he had hoped. Tom realized Jo was extremely smart and driven and always looking for a way out into the world.

He hesitantly agreed with Floyd's proposal, so long as Jo was satisfied and willing to give it a try. He had no illusions about the battle they would be fighting if accepted. Most of the military was in opposition to female cadets, and it wouldn't be an easy four years for Jo or Gina.

Now, time to talk to the girls.

Gina had been the first to speak after several minutes of stunned silence.

"You want us to join the military, and not just the military, but the military academy?" she squeaked.

"Dad, they don't even like women, much less want them to become officers. Why would you want me to do this?"

"Since Vietnam, most people my age don't like the government *or* the military. I mean, I don't talk about it, 'cause you're retired military, but a lot of us don't think we should have ever gone over there. Now you want me to join? Are you serious?"

Jo hadn't said anything. Tom looked over at his daughter. He saw the wheels turning. She was weighing the advantages as well as the possible cost to a "first" female cadet.

Gina continued to talk. "My grades aren't good enough for the Academy. I'm probably too little, and I don't want to be an Air Force Officer."

Still Jo said nothing.

On Gina went, "What did Mom say? Did you even talk to her? Does she want me to be an officer?"

Floyd spoke up at that point. "Yes, I talked to your mom, and no, she's not that thrilled. She said you wouldn't even consider it, that it would be too hard. She went through basic training, and it's not a walk in the park. Never mind the rigors of the Academy and the verbal abuse you might experience. But she made it, honey, and you can too. Yes, you'll have to really buckle down with the grades, that's true. But you have great athletic ability, both of you have been active in your community, you go to church and you've never been in any trouble. You're exactly what they're going to look for in that first class of female cadets. And, you're tough. You understand how to work, you've been part of a team…" He drifted off as he turned to look at Jo.

Jo, who had remained silent and near motionless throughout the exchange, began to tremble with excitement.

This was it. This was the way out.

"What do I have to do?" she said, and at that, it was Gina's turn to simply stand and stare.

Senior Year 1975-76

As the class of 1976 began their final year together, traditional roles for the girls graduating were changing just as drastically as the music and the clothes. Yesteryear's norms for women, to just become wives and mothers, raise children, and keep house were being shed by a new generation of ambitious and empowered women. These women were beginning to attend college in greater numbers. Their circle of influence was expanding into areas traditionally reserved for men. And it was in this sea of change that Jo and Gina tried to find their own paths.

One more trip to Little Rock, and a tradition between them would come to an end. Sure, there would be more shopping, but not for school--and this time, they got to drive themselves.

As she honked the horn for Jo, she thought about the many conversations she had had with her dad the last few weeks.

He was unbelievably serious when it came to the Academy. How could he even entertain the idea that she would wanna go through that? Didn't he remember how much trouble she had with reading, never mind math? *I can just imagine what that's gonna be like with all those guys that don't even want women there.* She shuddered.

At that moment, Jo ran out the front door.

"I'm coming! Hold ya' horses." She darted back in as the screen door slammed behind her.

Dammit, we're gonna get a late start. We won't have time to stop at that little café I like for lunch if she don't come on.

Another five minutes passed, and Gina honked again, this time several short bursts.

Jo came flying out, running the entire way to the end of the drive and hopping in the passenger seat.

"Hang on. I'm running late. I spent too long on the phone with Paul. He wanted us to pick up a box of labels the winery had printed in Little Rock, at some printing office downtown. I wrote down the name and stuck it in my purse. C'mon, let's go."

They let the top down, and the pedal too. If it was gonna be their last trip, it was gonna be a good one. They got to Little Rock by ten o'clock.

The first stop: Dillard's. They still loved the clothes and Jo still loved the escalator.

Six hours, twelve different bags, a box of labels, and lunch later, they were ready to come home.

The sun hung low in the sky, but still very visible, when they left Little Rock headed north. Two teenage girls, a rag-top Mustang, cool new clothes, and the open road. Bob Seger's "Like a Rock" rolled across the airwaves and out of the speakers. Jo looked inside her purse and pulled out a pack of Marlboro lights.

"You want one?"

"No, I don't like them. I don't understand why you do."

Jo ignored the remark.

"You realize this is the last time we're gonna get to shop for school."

"Yeah, and if my dad has his way, our next shopping spree will be in military duds."

"Yeah, I understand, and you spent a lot of your life moving from base to base. You know what's out there, but I don't. Really, what might be out there for me? I want a chance to try... to get out of this little bity town, and this might be my best shot. I wish you could find a way to 'want' to do this too, Gina."

"Well, I can't. You know how hard it is for me to study, to read? I can't see anything good when it comes to joining the military. Especially when you got to be 'the best and the brightest,' and we both know I'm not. What I really want to do is be with Robert, and if he gets a scholarship to South Arkansas University, I won't get to do that."

"That's not fair. You know how much he wants to go to college. He just wants to find a way outta' here, too."

"Oh, I know that, and I don't mean I don't want him to do it. It just isn't going to include me. Dad's not gonna let go of this. He's like a dog with a bone. He keeps gnawing at me, hopin' I'll change my mind."

"Well, you oughta think about it. I mean, what else do you wanna do?"

At that, Gina shrugged. She had no answer. She simply turned the volume up on the radio and smiled.

They were free as birds. Free as the sunshine that fell on them. Free as the auburn and blonde hair that swirled around their faces as they flew down the open road. Freedom… free to choose their path, free to live their life…

Wednesday morning, August 17th, was the first day back to school, their final school year. Their day began as it had for the last several years, with Louise driving them the first day. The girls were acutely aware that this would be the last time to return to these familiar halls.

In a school such as Polk Ridge, almost everyone knows everyone else. Most of the people they would graduate with had spent at least twelve years together, in one place, at one school. She had known these classmates her entire life. The one exception was Gina.

For Gina, she was sad to see it end. She'd given herself, without any kind of reservation, to this class and this school. Knowing that she wouldn't be leaving had allowed her to make friends and plans, and for once, truly fit in. She knew that if she took her dad's advice, she would once again be leaving. Leaving behind her friends and the life she had grown to love in Polk Ridge.

A strange, melancholy feeling crept into each girl as they walked down the hall for the first day of school. Jo was coping with the fact that she would never return to open another textbook and feed her hunger for knowledge. Gina was hit with the realization that it would be her last season to cheer for the Yellow Jackets and celebrate another winning season. Never mind the books--she wouldn't miss them.

The guys met them at the door to homeroom.

Robert and Gina had already been on campus for several weeks, with cheerleader and football practice.

For Jo and Paul, it was the first day back in several months. They'd spent quite a lot of weekend time together over the summer, and Paul finally felt comfortable whenever Jo walked up. They had so much in common; they both worked for their dads, they spent their summers immersed in their family businesses, and they both excelled in their classes. He already realized he loved her, he just couldn't find a way to say it.

"Hey ladies." Paul was the first to speak, his voice much deeper now than when he had first met Gina. No more squeaking.

"Hey Paul," they chimed together.

"What are we doin' Friday night after the game, girls? The old iron bridge?"

"Yeah," Gina answered for them both. "You and Jo workin' the concession stand? If so, we'll leave from here after Robert changes."

The first game of the season was at home, and Paul and Jo worked the concession stand as usual.

"Of course. We'll wait for ya'll in the parking lot."

"We've got a whole year to plan. I may not have gone to school here all my life, but I don't want them to forget Gina Ingram anytime soon." She giggled as they made their way into homeroom. It definitely would be a year to remember.

Football season roared to life with a bang, and the Yellow Jackets won their first three games: two at home and one away. Polk Ridge

High School was a 1A school, which meant that most of the team played offense and defense. Robert played as a fullback on offense and a linebacker on defense.

What they lacked in numbers, they certainly didn't lack in spirit. Every Friday night was packed with screaming crowds. Friday night football was the main attraction in their small town.

Gina was in heaven. She cheered and screamed while Robert blocked and ran. Jo and Paul watched from the concession stand. They didn't understood the fascination with, or purpose of, lining up against someone just to be knocked down and stomped on, and then get up and do it again.

The fourth game of the season was against the Ponca Indians, and the game was at home. Tied with only two minutes left in the game, Jo couldn't even hear the customer's requests at the concession stand because of the cheering fans.

This is ridiculous. How can anybody get so worked up over a game?

For three plays, they scrimmaged but never moved. The Yellow Jackets weren't gaining ground, and the Indians weren't losing any. With twenty-two seconds left on the clock, they got ready for the last play. The Yellow Jackets were in blue and gold, the Indians in red and white. It was third and seven on the thirty-six-yard line. The Indians outweighed and outmanned them, but the Yellow Jackets hung on like a rusty nail. The ball snapped, and every fan held their breath. The announcer's voice boomed over the loud speakers.

"The ball is snapped, and it's handed off… handed off… handed off to number 24, folks…"

It was a sea of meshed blue, gold, red, and white. Out of this confusion, number 24 emerged, hugging a pigskin. Robert had the ball and ran his heart out. The announcer bellowed once again—

"He's at the thirty, now the twenty-five, he's at the tweeenty…"

The roar was deafening.

"Now at the fifteen… crossing the ten... touchdown, Yellow Jackets!"

There wasn't a band to play, but with the noise on the field, you wouldn't have heard them anyway. Even Jo and Paul mustered some excitement over this play. They couldn't hear each other but they could nod and grin.

This was gonna be some kind of celebration night!

The Old Iron Bridge would be packed. Robert and Gina would be the center of attention, and Jo and Paul would be right there with them to celebrate.

On Monday morning, the remnants of Friday night's spirit still lingered, and everybody at school talked about Robert's amazing play. Robert and Gina basked in their victory.

For Jo and Paul, their victories weren't hammered out on a field, but rather in the classroom. They were competing for the valedictorian position, and although they were dating, they took their rivalry very seriously.

As Jo made her way to the library to meet with the annual staff, Paul stopped her in the hall.

"You know we're tied right now for the spot, right?"

"Yeah, but we've still got the end of the year to go, and I will win, Paul. You just wait and see."

"You really want this, don't you?"

"Of course I do, but I wanna win fair and square. It's no good if you don't give it your best shot, you understand me? I don't wanna win cause you want me to. I wanna win because I did better than you."

"I'm not gonna let you win, because if you do, I'll never live it down. I can hear my ol' man saying 'Paul, I can't believe you let some girl beat you;' oh, no, I'm not gonna listen to that."

"You might have to, especially if you don't pull that chemistry grade up past an 88. Mine's 92--gotcha beat so far."

"I got time. But what I don't have time to do is talk to you. What you doin' after the annual staff meeting?"

"Not much. Gotta run by the co-op and then go home. Why?"

"Meet me at the bridge around 5 p.m. We really need to talk before graduation."

"Graduation? Now? Why?"

Paul gave her that *not here* look.

"Okay. See ya then."

Now what did he want to say at the bridge that he couldn't say here? She would never understand men.

Paul's great-great-granddaddy had moved to the Ozarks in 1838, right after Arkansas became a state. He bought one hundred and sixty acres above the Buffalo River, right outside of town. The sandy soil and hills of Polk Ridge were great for raising grapes, and for making wine. And since that time, the Collection family had been producing and selling some of Arkansas's finest.

The family business had been in operation one hundred and thirty-five years, even during the Prohibition, when it was illegal to make and sell any kind of alcohol. The first Paul Collection (1908 – 1962) had devised a plan that worked long enough to keep them in business by selling medicinal wine to local doctors and sacramental wine to the Catholic churches in Arkansas and southern Missouri. It wasn't the most profitable of times, but they managed to survive.

Not everyone in Polk County agreed with the making and drinking of wine. There had been more than one occasion when young Paul felt the sting of criticism from his peers and adults alike. He had learned to simply accept the fact that not everyone will agree with your choices. You must do what you have to do. And in his case, it was making wine.

Julie and Mark Collection, Paul's parents, now owned and ran the entire operation. Paul, even at a young age, had been expected to participate in the family business. Much akin to Jo, his summers were spent working in the vineyards and winery, leaving little time for summer recreation.

He wasn't going to school on a scholarship, and he would never be "Mr. Athlete," but he was a handsome teenager that needed a little extra time to grow into a handsome man, and he wanted Jo to hang around for the process. He was intelligent, with great character, manners, and a good solid upbringing. Characteristics that most young women of the Ozarks would find attractive. He wasn't interested in most women--only one.

It was almost 5:30 p.m. before Paul made it to the bridge. Jo was ready to leave and go home.

"Where have you been? I thought you said 5?"

Boy, that's just what I need. I'm about to die from nervousness, and now she's irritated, thought Paul.

"I'm sorry. I did say 5, but my dad wouldn't let me leave the counter 'til 5, so that's why I'm late."

"It's alright. I needed a few minutes to myself anyway. What did you wanna talk about graduation for? It's still months away."

"It's not really graduation I wanted to talk about." He paused for a minute. "Jo, we've been dating for a while now, and I've known you most of my life, and...I need to tell you something." *Crap, this isn't the way I wanted it go.*

"Listen," he continued, "we have so much in common. You love learning as much as I do, and you're so smart and funny, and you're almost the prettiest girl I've ever seen, but..."

"I thought I *was* the prettiest girl you'd ever seen," she laughed. "C'mon, Paul, what are you trying to say? You tired of datin' me?"

"No! I'm trying to tell you I love you…" And just as quickly as he spit it out, he stopped. He felt the color rush to his face.

"Ever since I kissed you, I've been falling in love with you. I know you want to leave Polk Ridge and do something with your life. But we could do so much here. You could do so much with me. I just want you to know how I feel and ask you if you feel the same way. I need to know you'll be a part of my life, even after we graduate."

His heart hammered in his chest. He looked at Jo, his eyes pleading for a response. He needed her to say "I love you too, Paul."

"Oh, Paul." Her heart was breaking for him, just as she could tell his was shattering to pieces the longer she waited.

"Paul, I can't… I can't tell you I love you and then leave. You're tied to this place forever. Your future is with your family's business. Mine isn't here, and I'm never gonna be happy just being somebody's wife, not even yours. I don't know exactly what I feel for you; I love going out with you, I love how we talk, I love to be with you, but I don't love you enough to stay. I can't. I gotta know what's out there… and you won't go."

When she finished, Paul's face had crumpled. His eyes brimmed with tears. Several seconds passed before he spoke, in a voice that was low and pleading.

"I can wait, Jo. I can wait 'til you see what you gotta see if you can just tell me you'll come back. I can wait for you."

CHAPTER 4

The Letters

THE END OF OCTOBER was approaching, and Halloween. It was their favorite school holiday for one reason: the Halloween Costume Ball.

Every year, students were allowed to run for King and Queen of their class, and winners would be acknowledged at the Halloween Ball. Then, out of those winners, a King and Queen of the Ball would be chosen. Popularity determined the winners.

Jo never thought about competing for Queen, but Gina always entered the contest for the envied position. This year proved no different. Jo was only ever concerned with winning the costume competition. This was the only popularity contest she ever entered--and she entered year after year.

Everybody got to design a costume and wear it. After the King and Queen's election, teachers would judge the best costume, and some lucky student would receive the "High School Horror Award." This was *her* specialty—the more grotesque, the better. She'd won every year since ninth grade. If she won this year, she could leave her alma mater with the additional title of "most wins ever by one student."

For this year's costume, she needed to enlist Robert's help. While

Gina busied herself preparing a queen's gown, she made a costume based on the Stephen King novel *Carrie*. She'd finished reading the book a couple of months ago and planned to dress up as Carrie for the Costume Ball. She was "gonna knock 'em dead."

"Robert," Jo said as she stopped him in the hallway Monday afternoon before the ball. "I need some help from you with my Halloween costume and entrance into the ball next week. Will you have some time this afternoon to let me explain and see if you can lend a hand?"

"Sure, but it'll have to be after practice. It's over around 6:30 and I'm usually out of the dressing room by 7. This is not gonna get me in trouble with, say, the principal, or your mom and dad? Is it, Jo?"

"Why, Robert, how could you even think such a thing? Would I ever do anything to get you into any trouble?" And with that, she displayed a grin that reached from ear to ear.

"Nooo, absolutely not, Jo. Not you!" he teased, returning the same expansive grin.

After clearing up that one small issue, she proceeded to the bus, and he went out the school's back doors to the gym where they dressed for practice. Both of them knew there was a definite possibility that someone would most likely be in *some kind* of trouble after the costume ball. They just didn't realize how much.

The Halloween King and Queen's Ball was always held on a Saturday night because of the football games on Friday night. Gina was totally immersed in the final touches of her Queen's gown (she had, as usual, won the senior class nomination). She didn't notice her best friend's or her boyfriend's absence.

Saturday, at precisely 2 p.m., Jo and Robert slid through the backdoor to the auditorium. On Monday, right before she talked to Robert, Jo had attached a length of rope to one of the rafters that hovered high above the stage. No one, not even the nosy janitor, had noticed. Today they were gonna practice, just to make sure that her idea would work.

It took almost an hour, but it worked beautifully.

"Jo, it's gonna be automatic detention time over this."

"No, we'll probably get suspended over this. But oh my, what a grand sight it will be! Do not say a word. Tonight, when they get the contestants on stage, you hide behind this curtain, in case somethin' does go wrong. I already asked Ms. Barkley to save me for last. I told her it was because I've won so many times, I hope the judges will see somebody else they like first." She giggled. "I don't think they stand a chance!"

No one, not even Gina, was prepared for the final entrance Jo made, and had it not been for Robert's quick thinking, Jo wouldn't have been ready either.

She climbed to the top of a ladder he had placed for her behind the curtain on the left side of the stage. She grabbed the rope, hung a few days earlier, and prepared to make her entrance. Just as all the Costume contestants finished lining the stage, and she heard Ms. Barkley call her name, Jo let herself go. Free falling over the heads of the other contestants.

She flew, dressed in an old ball gown, covered in fake blood, and painted with white face paint that made her appear ghostly, as though she were "risen from the dead."

Everyone looked and gasped in horror. She was midway over the stage when the rafter creaked and then snapped. It had worked fine during the practice run, but it was so old, and the strain of a second flight proved to be too much.

And just as she magically appeared, she began to fall. Her blood-curdling scream wasn't the moaning wail she had practiced earlier. It was the scream of a girl in trouble.

Robert, who had an uneasiness over the whole entrance idea from the start, was positioned behind the stage curtains to the right of the stage. As he realized Jo was in real trouble, he darted out to break her fall. Instead of an awkward save, he managed to catch her quite gracefully, almost as if it were a practiced event.

One of the contestants fainted. Three bolted and ran.

Needless to say, everything came to a screeching halt, and not one judge was in the mood to give Jo her coveted award.

As soon as the stage was cleared and the audience recovered, the Ball was declared over. There were several people in the principal's office waiting to see Jo and Robert. It seemed there was some explaining to do.

On October 7, 1975, President Ford signed the Defense Authorization Bill of 1976 and it was put into law. Women are now finally allowed to be cadets.

Jo had not forgotten one single word of Floyd's proposal; it seemed as though Gina tried really hard *to forget.*

Now that it was law, he intended to contact an old friend and request an appointment to meet with him. He wanted military, as well as congressional, nominations for the girls.

Floyd spent many hours on the phone that summer preparing for every possibility, talking with old friends and requesting letters of support and recommendation. Nothing about this was concrete until signed by President Ford, but he wasn't going to wait until the last minute to prepare. He left nothing to chance--nothing except Gina's agreement to go. He was still hoping Jo could talk Gina into at least applying.

As November began, he was on the phone again *and* on the road. The girls met the eligibility requirements: they were at least seventeen before entering the academy, U.S. citizens, and of course unmarried with no dependents.

He approached his daughter several times in late October and once again in early November. She and Robert had been spending a great deal of time together. And although Floyd liked him and believed that he had a bright future, it would be *after* he graduated from college, not before. It was with these thoughts that he tried to persuade her once more.

"Gina, I know you're tired of this conversation, but I want to ask you something, something I don't think you've given any thought. If you actually want to make a life with Robert, how are you going to do that?"

"What do you mean by 'how'?"

"Well, it used to be pretty easy to live life like your mom and I.

But nowadays, lots of women are working. It takes money to buy a house, cars, clothes, and raise children. Have you talked with Robert about any of this? Have you made any plans?"

"No, he's goin' to college, or at least he wants to go to college, and his coach is tryin' to get him a baseball scholarship."

"Well, if you aren't sure about you *and* Robert, what plans have you made for you without him after graduation?"

Gina paused. She hadn't made any. She had given thought to becoming a flight attendant, but she didn't have the first idea how to apply, and she didn't want to share this with her dad anyway.

She sighed. *Just go ahead and say yes. Besides, those physicals aren't until March. A lot may change between now and March, and it won't hurt to agree. I'm really tired of talking about this.*

"Alright, I'll try. I don't know what I'm gonna do after graduation, and I might as well try this, especially since Jo's goin'."

He smiled. Finally, common sense prevailed.

He took them to Little Rock, the closest recruiting office, and they met with their Liaison Officer, Lt. Col John Listermann on November 10th.

Lt. Col. Listermann was a balding man in his late forties, with a pleasant disposition and two daughters of his own. Much to Floyd's surprise, they weren't met with staunch opposition. In fact, the Lt. Col. supported the legislation.

"Ya know, Mr. Ingram, I've had a good life in the military. I'd like for my daughters to be able to pursue military careers as well. This legislation, although heavily opposed by some in the military, will pave the way for that possibility. Y'all have as much support as I can give."

And with that, the process was underway.

Since it wasn't until October when female cadets could legally apply for admission to the academy, the status of "pre-candidate" had been applied to the several hundred female applicants until a final determination was made in April. This meant *all* paperwork must be complete and ready for submission by December 31st.

Obstacle number one placed in the path of female applicants.

Gina and Jo were given packets of information and instructions. There were form letters that had to be completed by their Congressman, teacher evaluations, transcript requests for the school, a pre-candidate questionnaire, writing samples, and extracurricular activities records for them to complete. Once completed, they would make another trip to Little Rock to submit everything to the Lieutenant Colonel. He would schedule their personal interview during that trip.

He, along with a panel of five additional Air Force officers, would conduct the interview. It would be difficult, he explained, and they needed to prepare for some hostility. Most USAF Officers opposed the admission of female cadets. Once the interview was complete sometime in late January, the girls must complete the medical examination.

They had to schedule a fitness assessment with a coach at their school. The forms he or she needed to complete were included in the packets they received and bring the completed fitness forms with them when they got their medical evaluations.

"Once that is complete, I submit this information to the Air Force Academy in Colorado Springs, Colorado," said the colonel. "And we wait. Final determination will be made in late April. You will receive either an acceptance or rejection letter by May 31st. Any questions?"

He gave them a grin that seemed to say, "Why, of course you have questions. Who wouldn't?"

Once they were back home, Floyd put together a checklist of the many materials they needed to complete and worked closely with them to gather the information.

He went to school and requested their transcripts. He gave the teachers the evaluation forms. The girls had more than enough to do in completing the questionnaires, writing samples, and extracurricular activities records.

Jo tackled her forms with zeal as though her entire future hinged on this one opportunity. Gina, still not very receptive to the idea of a military life, gave it a half-hearted effort.

Finally, on December 16th, everything was complete, and they made one more trip to Little Rock. This time, Tom accompanied them. As the last couple of months had passed, both fathers began to see this great opportunity come to life, and each man was filled with unbelievable pride at the thought of his daughter being one of the first females accepted into the academy.

Now, they waited.

While they waited, there were two things that consumed Gina's life: Robert and cheering. She loved the excitement of cheering at games—the lights, competing teams, screaming crowds and Robert. Although football season was over, basketball was beginning, and games were on Tuesdays and Thursdays, beginning right after Christmas. The holidays this year heralded not only a change in sports, but a change in relationships. Christmas that year brought her a present she never expected.

Robert had just pulled up and was at a lope as he crossed the yard. He came to eat supper with Gina and her parents and hopefully spend some time alone with Gina. He had only a few weeks earlier gotten his own ride, a '56 Chevy. Almost always in need of some kind of repair, and with gears that inevitably failed to work without roadside assistance from Robert, it was at least a way to get around. Any truck was better than no truck.

"Hey, baby. It's Christmas Eve, and I got somethin' for ya," said Robert.

She giggled, and called out from the front porch, "What ya got for me, Robert Phillips? A bag of switches?"

"No, much better than switches." And he stopped to plant a kiss, along with that look that made her knees knock and her heart melt.

He tapped his right jeans pocket. "Right here. Right here's the gift. But you gotta wait 'til after supper."

It was almost impossible to wait.

"I can't. Let me have it now."

"Nope. Gotta wait." And he ducked inside.

"Hey, Mrs. Ingram. I've been looking forward to that Christmas ham all day. Thanks for inviting me over."

And with that, Gina was forced to wait. And wait and wait…

Finally, around 8 p.m., Robert asked her parents if they could go out for a while and cruise around town. He wanted to look at the Christmas decorations and lights with Gina that sparkled bright red, blue and white throughout most of the town.

As they went outside to leave, Robert stopped to check the gears on the old truck and then got inside.

She slid into the seat beside him, and he backed out of the drive.

"Okay, I've been patient. Can I have it now?"

"You look nice, Gina. That new sweater Jo gave you for Christmas really suits that blonde hair and those beautiful blue eyes."

"Quit stalling, Robert. Let me have it."

He kept talking.

"Ya know, any guy in town would be proud to date a girl like you. You're athletic, you're funny, you look great in a pair of jeans…"

"C'mon, Robert. Please."

During their drive, they'd been steadily making their way to the Old Iron Bridge.

He pulled the truck to a stop on the banks of the Buffalo River and cut the engine and lights. Now he looked at her through the moonlight.

"You really are a beautiful woman."

"Oh, Robert." She reached over to kiss him, the soft look of love glowing in her eyes.

He reached into his left pocket.

"That's not where my gift is."

"Oh, I know that. I brought you this chain my momma gave me. You've been wearing my class ring on your finger, and it's too big. I asked her if she could give me a chain for you to put the ring on. This was her momma's."

It was a tiny silver chain for a tiny neck. He opened the clasp, put the ring on the chain, and then fastened it around her neck.

He'd given her the ring during the summer when he asked her to go steady. Set with a stone that reflected the royal blue of the school's colors and engraved on the side with *"Today's Dreams are Tomorrow's Future,"* it was his most shining achievement. It swelled him with pride to know he was the first in his family to graduate and wear a class ring. It was a ring that Gina had worn with pride. For her, it symbolized the love they shared.

"Okay, *now* can I have my present?"

He reached into his pocket and retrieved the small little box.

"Close your eyes and give me your hand."

Gina did as she was told. He placed the gift into her palm.

"Open them." Her eyes widened at the sight of the tiny diamond set in a band of gold.

"Oh, Robert. Oh my gosh!"

For once, she was speechless. She sat for several seconds just staring at the ring, then at Robert. Of all the things she thought the gift might be, a diamond ring had never crossed her mind.

Even though he was nervous, Robert didn't dance around his question.

"Gina, would you consider gettin' engaged? We've been dating for a while now, and I wanna make it a little more permanent. Who knows what might happen in the next few months. My scholarship, your application to the academy… a lot is changing and I wanna know you'll be a part of my life. My whole life, not just the next few months."

His eyes were twinkling, and his face was overtaken by his smile, but his heart was jumping out of his chest.

So, whatta you say?"

She continued to stare at the ring.

"Well?" His heart hammered. *What if she's gonna say no?*

"Yes!...Yes! Oh my, yes!"

Gina was head over hills in love with Robert Phillips. She loved everything about him.

He was a great athlete, playing not only football, but also basketball and baseball. During their senior year, if there was an athletic event, they were both there – she cheering and Robert playing. And he was solid, dependable, kind. Who could ask for anything better? He made her heart race, yet she felt so safe with him.

His family had lived in Polk Ridge for over a hundred years, farming the foothills of the Ozarks, working in the sawmills, and playing music in their spare time. Since he came from a large family, it seemed he was forever in search of a younger brother or sister that had decided to spend the afternoon playing hooky from chores or school. It was the relationship with his siblings that amazed her most.

She was impressed with not only his character, but his closeness with his siblings. She had none, and no way to understand the ties that bind brother and sister, or brother and brother. She was at a loss to understand. Jo was as close as she had ever come to having a sibling tie to anyone, and after watching Robert and his brothers, she wasn't too sure that it even came close.

His parents, Ellie and Ira, were farming folks, and as such placed no great emphasis on educating their bunch. They were more interested in their ability to stay healthy and help out at the farm. Recreational time was often dictated by the weather or the lack of funds to accommodate such a large brood and this is where their music, musical talents, and love of each other saw them through many otherwise bleak times.

His mom played piano and made sure that she took the time to instruct each of her children in the reading and playing of music on the piano. His dad was a fiddle player, and as soon as Robert could hold the fiddle, he had passed on his own musical instruction. All ten of the Phillips children could play some kind of instrument, and most could actually carry a tune. Robert was one of the few with absolutely no ability to sing. He did, however, have one exceptional talent: he was a great athlete. And it was this ability that would hopefully be his ticket out of town to a better, more prosperous life.

Besides his athletics, he actually excelled at school academically. His mom often laughed and said she had no idea where he got his smarts; it certainly wasn't from her, and judging from his dad, who followed family tradition sawmilling and farming, it wasn't from him either. When he wasn't chasing a sibling, he was inclined to spend most of his time with either a ball or a book. The books were paying off, and he managed to maintain A's and B's throughout high school. When he began to date Gina, he insisted that she study and continue her education after high school. Gina, ever stubborn at continuing in school for one minute longer than was absolutely necessary, flatly refused to think about college. The only way she would ever see a college campus would be because of Robert, not because she enrolled as a student.

As the oldest, Robert was often in charge of his siblings when they were away from their mom and dad; this responsibility had produced a very dependable, caring young man. One that Gina had fallen hopelessly in love with. But Robert's plans after high school might not include her, at least not the way she hoped. She knew he loved her, but he wasn't going to give up college--not for her, not for anyone. It was his way out.

On January 22nd, the phone rang, and Gina picked it up. The man on the other end asked for Floyd Ingram, so she called out to her dad, who was sitting in the living room.

"Telephone, Dad."

He made his way gingerly to the kitchen.

Maybe it was Little Rock. Hopefully, it was Lt .Col Listermann, with good news.

"Hello?"

"Hello, Mr. Ingram. This is Lt. Col Listermann. I received confirmation to schedule Gina and Jo's interview and medical evaluation. They need to meet me here, at the recruiting office at 0900, on March 7th. The panel interview will take place at 10 a.m., and then I'll instruct them concerning the medical exam - where and what to expect. They will, of course, need to sign a release, and they also need to bring their fitness evaluation. By the way, I have no news as of yet from the academy concerning the status of the application, only approval to proceed with interviews and evaluations. And going forward, my communication will be strictly with the girls, you understand?"

"Oh, yes. Completely. That's how it should be. I'll have them there. Thank you for calling." Floyd hung up the phone. He was hoping for more exciting news.

The fitness evaluation was scheduled for the last Saturday in February, and both girls were more than a little nervous.

Jo, although she had almost certainly secured the valedictorian position, wasn't an athlete. She could only hope that those afternoon hikes in the Ozarks paid off. And, although she was completely exhausted from the effort, Jo passed her fitness exam.

Gina, on the other hand, flew through her evaluation. It wasn't the fitness issue that gave her a problem; it had been those stupid questionnaires.

The following Saturday, they were in Little Rock, reporting for their interview and medical exam. As they finished their final leg of the process and returned to the recruiting office, paperwork in hand, Lt. Col. Listermann sat down with each of them, alone.

Floyd never asked what he said. He didn't need to. Their faces clearly displayed what he had known.

They'd received their first taste of military life. The colonel, simply out of worry and concern for the atmosphere they would enter at an Academy that was extremely resentful of females, took it upon himself to explain some of the language and hostility they might encounter. If they were going to withdraw, now should be the time.

Jo, with her stubborn pride and driving desire to escape, never wavered. Gina, on the other hand, wasn't so sure, but she didn't withdraw.

It would only be a few short weeks before each girl received an answer. For Jo, it seemed an eternity. And for Gina, the answer would come too soon. All of this work culminated into one brief letter of explanation; a simple "yes" or "no" would be the answer to their months of work—either accepted or rejected.

A single one-page letter would be the impetus that altered the course of life for them.

Spring Break 1976

On the heels of the application process for the academy came spring break for Polk Ridge. For the senior class, their last.

Spring break always heralded the end of a normally long, cold winter, and everyone in Polk Ridge, from adults to children, were ready for outdoor activities.

The senior class planned a weeklong trip to the Crater of Diamonds State Park. Everyone had heard the story of the diamond mine in Murfreesboro and were proud to claim rights since Arkansas is the only location in the United States where you can find blue-white diamonds.

The thought of a new adventure seemed to lift Gina's spirits, and the impending letter was pushed to the back of her mind. She just refused to think about the academy.

If I don't think about it, maybe, just maybe, I won't have to go.

The entire class participated in the planning, and each day's events were carefully laid out, scheduled weeks in advance. They were leaving the Saturday before spring break and returning on the following Friday. Two teachers, Miss Barkley and Mr. Thomson, as well as several parents chaperoned the trip, and everyone looked forward to a chance of finding a real diamond.

The Crater of Diamonds State Park is the only diamond-producing place in the world, open to the public, and located close to the Little Missouri River. So not only can you dig for diamonds, but you can also fish, camp, and hike—everything that the girls could ask for in adventure.

The winter of 1975-76 brought so many changes for the girls. Not only were they finishing their last year of high school, but Gina was experiencing her first taste of real love, and Jo was experiencing the bitterness of a first failed relationship. It was an emotional roller-coaster for them.

Since their conversation at the bridge, Paul had shied away from Jo. They weren't dating anymore, and it seemed even the competition for the position of valedictorian had lost prominence in his life. There was also the normal activity at school: annual staff, debate team, and Beta Club. Jo just wanted to spend a few days doing nothing but having fun. Surely that would help her feel like her old self.

For Gina, she'd been on an emotional high for most of the year. Her relationship with Robert was great. Although the stormclouds were gathering, she took the same approach she'd taken with the academy application: she just didn't think about it. Other than the slight case of spring fever and laziness she seemed to have, she had had a wonderful winter and looked so forward to finding another diamond to match the one on her finger.

Saturday arrived with a glorious purple-and-pink sunrise, and the yellow bus, packed with teenagers, teachers and parents, lumbered away from the school at exactly 6 a.m.

"Hey, Gina, what did you say we were doing tomorrow?"

Robert hadn't taken the time to worry about the week's scheduled events. Gina would tell him, play by play.

"We're supposed to meet at 9 a.m. in front of the mine shaft building for instructions on mining. One of the park attendants will show us where we can mine, what we might find, and explain the different tools we can use to dig. It's supposed to take a couple of hours, then we're free to do whatever we want until Monday morning."

"Cool. Anybody wanna hike tomorrow afternoon?" He was looking at one of the brochures they'd received. "They got some great lookin' trails."

There were at least fifteen others who wanted to go, and even Paul, who wasn't sitting anywhere close to Jo and sat with Shelly toward the back of the bus, raised his hand to be included.

It was painfully evident to everyone, especially Jo, that things weren't ever going to be the same with Paul, or for that matter, with Gina and Robert. The four of them had had a wonderful time last summer, full of mischief and falling in love. That, however, was gone. The reality of senior year ending and upcoming adulthood cast a melancholy spell on the teenagers.

They got there late Saturday afternoon. Once unpacking was finished, cabins were assigned. After supper, it was lights out. On Sunday morning, they got their education in mining and hiked in the afternoon. On Monday morning, however, the digging began in earnest.

The park attendant showed them the field that had been prepared for them and that he could be located over at the guardhouse if they found anything or needed to weigh a stone. With that, he wished them happy hunting and went inside. The newly constructed guardhouse had air conditioning, and he wasn't going to waste one precious minute of it.

Competition erupted between the boys and girls. It only took a few minutes for the girls to take the left side of the field, guys on the right. And the race was on.

As usual, Jo took the lead. "C'mon, Gloria. You and Judy and Gina, come with me. Let's start over here by this low spot. It looks like a great place."

They began to dig, sift, and look for anything that remotely resembled a colored stone. Jo just wanted to find something, anything.

Morning turned to midday, and midday to early afternoon. Not one diamond was found. They found amethyst, jasper, garnet, and peridot, and Robert even managed to find a snake, but no diamonds.

Around 4 p.m., hot and tired of digging, Floyd called out to the "miners".

"Okay, ladies and gentlemen, time to call it quits. We've had a great day, but we need to get ready for supper. We have reservations in town tonight, so let's pack up our stuff and get ready to turn it in to the guardhouse."

As they gathered their tools and prepared to go, Paul quietly continued to dig. He'd picked a spot on the very outskirts of the field, working with Robert and David. Suddenly, Robert let out a low whistle, and everybody stopped to turn and look.

"Hey, Mr. Ingram, can you come over here just a minute?"

As Floyd walked up, he could see the huge stone in the palm of Paul's hand.

"Well, I'll be, son. I think you finally found one. Let's take it over to the guardhouse."

As they reached the guardhouse, even the park attendant stared in awe. It was huge *and* white. Or at least, it would be. Right now, it was covered in dirt and had a milky appearance.

"I believe you've found yourself a beauty, son. That's gotta be at least five carats. Come on in, and we'll weigh it and see."

Sure enough, it was 5.37 carats, and a true white diamond. Paul rolled it around in his fingers. He wasn't too sure how, but he did have an idea when it came to *what* he was going to do with it. He folded it into the small piece of cloth the attendant had given him.

They continued to dig at intervals throughout the week, but nothing they found compared to Paul's diamond. Almost everyone had given up on the quest for the diamond and filled their week with other activities. There was one activity noticeably absent though.

On their final night, Gina couldn't take it anymore.

"Jo, we've been here this whole week, and we haven't done one thing to prank anybody. You losing your edge?"

"No, I haven't felt like pranking this week. You got any ideas? We still got tonight."

"As a matter of fact, I do. I bought this little green plastic snake while we were in town Monday, and I've just left it in my suitcase. Did you see Mr. Thomson when Robert found that real snake? He 'bout jumped out of his skin. Reckon what he'd do if one showed up in his bed?"

Jo laughed. She already knew they were going to find out in just a matter of a few hours.

As everybody else filed out for supper, Jo and Gina made their way quietly over to Mr. Thomson's cabin. The door wasn't locked, and they slipped inside. In less than ten minutes, they joined everybody else for supper, eating and waiting.

It was dusky dark by the time everyone finished, cleaned up, and made their way to their cabins. Jo and Gina waited outside. It was time.

They watched as Mr. Thomson entered his cabin. He didn't bother to turn on any lights, simply undressing in the dark and hopping into bed.

The moment he reached for the covers and slid into a comfortable position, he felt the sleek coolness of something foreign against his thigh. He froze. The old mattress was lumpy, and because of the weight of his body, it created a valley where he lay. At that same moment, the cold, smooth object shifted against his thigh. The shrieking, yelping, and wailing that ensued sent them rolling in laughter.

Thanks to the feel of the snake, the dark cabin, and the fact that he wasn't much of an outdoorsman, he was certain he was going to die.

And so were Jo and Gina, from laughter.

CHAPTER 5

Their Senior Year is about to end.
Letters are going to arrive.
Graduation speeches are going to be given.
Changes are about to come to Polk Ridge.

March faded into April.

THE 5TH WAS THE cutoff for tallying grades to determine the valedictorian. Jo sensed it was going to be close, so very close.

The fierce competition she and Paul shared when they were dating had intensified in the last few months. He had bested her in history and English. She had him in science and math.

It was gonna come down to their elective classes. They had both chosen chemistry and PE. And since neither one was an athlete, chemistry was going to be the deciding grade.

Mr. Taylor was the high school principal, and on Friday, April 5th, he came over the loudspeaker in their English class.

"Miss Meadows, do you have Jo Felsenthal and Paul Collections in your class?"

"Yessir, they're here."

"Please send them to the office for a few minutes?"

Jo's heart beat so hard she could see her shirt move.

Paul looked calmly straight ahead as they made their way to the office. He said nothing.

"Paul, before we go in, I wanna tell you something."

"Okay."

So impersonal, so detached. She faltered. This was because of her, not the competition. Because of what she didn't tell him at the bridge, not because she might win.

"If I lose, it's been an honor to compete against someone as great as you. And if you lose, I hope you'll think the same way."

"What I "think" doesn't really matter. It's only whether you win or lose, Jo."

He opened the door and stepped inside, leaving the door open for her, waiting on her.

Somehow, win or lose, it wasn't going to be the sweet victory she had envisioned.

April turned into May

Graduation was in two weeks. Letters from the academy were supposed to arrive any day. Senior trip was coming up in early June. Life was speeding forward.

It was Friday, May 3rd. The final bell of the day rang, and teenagers, children, and teachers burst forth from every corner of Polk Ridge High School.

Only one more week to go! Graduation was going to be held the Friday after school was out, and the halls of this grand old lady would close to Jo and Gina forever. Each girl had mixed thoughts and emotions, for different reasons.

"Jo, you wanna come over and let's ride around? Robert's gotta meet with Coach Fleming. Something about a scholarship he's tryin' to get to South Arkansas University."

"Sure, but I gotta go by the house first. I wanna check the mail."

"You worried about that letter, ain't you? I hope the answer is no."

"Gina, don't say that. How can you want that? We won't ever get another chance that compares to this. The first female cadets--you know what that can mean?"

"I don't care what it might mean. I don't wanna go. I'm gonna ask Robert if I can go with him. I can get a job doin' somethin' while he goes to college."

"Sure you can. Where you gonna live? In your car?"

"No, I'm gonna live with him. He can get an apartment instead of livin' in the dorms. I know it'll cost a little more, but I can work and help pay for it."

"You gotta be kiddin' me. You know what you're daddy's gonna say and *do*?" You can just forget *livin'* with anybody." She emphasized the "livin'".

"Whatever… just come on over to the house, and don't say anything about what I wanna do to Mom or Dad, not even by accident. I'm gonna take a nap while I'm waitin' on you. I've been so damned sleepy lately."

"Too many late nights with Robert, huh?"

Forty-five minutes later, Jo pulled into the drive, right behind Robert, except he pulled in like the devil was chasing him.

"What's wrong with…?" And her voice trailed. He looked as though he was going to laugh and cry all at once.

"Where's Gina? Inside?" He was practically shouting.

"Yeah, but she's probably asleep. She said she was gonna take a nap."

"Well, she's gotta get up for this." He waved papers like a mad man.

He took the yard in three strides and bounded through the door. "Gina! Gina!"

She stumbled into the kitchen from the living room, sleep still visible on her face, but as she looked at Robert and then the papers he was holding, she was immediately wide awake. "What is that?"

His hands trembled as he opened the letter to show her. She had never seen him so overcome with emotion, not even when he gave her his ring. He was bursting with excitement. She looked at the paper. The letterhead was stamped in bold, maroon letters: "South Arkansas University."

She started reading, and before she finished, he tossed her into the air and swung her around.

"I got a *full* scholarship! A baseball scholarship! I got it! I got it!"

He let out some kind of holler that sent Jo and Gina into peals of laughter.

"You're crazy, Robert Phillips." It was Jo that spoke. "But I'm so happy for you. You got your ticket, now use it!"

That Friday night, all of them--even Paul--celebrated Robert's scholarship. The day was stamped into Gina's memory forever; he was so happy, so excited, and so full of hope as they celebrated his future. One down, two to go.

Wednesday, May 15

Two days until graduation. Jo's valedictorian speech was ready; she had practiced until she had it memorized. Paul would deliver the Salutatorian's address, and although her vision of this moment didn't in the end resemble reality, she was ready. Ready to move on. She needed that letter. That most important ticket out.

As valedictorian, she had received offers from several of the major universities in Arkansas and most of the community colleges. She let those letters pile up in her room. She wanted *the* letter. The one from the Academy.

School let out at lunch, primarily because there was nothing else for the students to learn. Semester exams were finished, and the seniors had already practiced for graduation in the auditorium. Those seemed like very good reasons to call off the school day at 12 so that's what they did.

Practice lasted until 2, and Miss Meadows met with them to discuss their senior trip. The senior trip to Little Rock to visit the capital was a tradition at Polk Ridge High School.

Mr. Hays, the first principal at the school when it was established in 1922, had felt that no Arkansans' education was complete until the student had visited the capital in Little Rock. He had written a letter to each graduating class every year until his retirement in 1938. The last letter he wrote had been published and given to each and every graduating class thereafter.

In his letter, he thanked them for attending Polk Ridge, explaining that as a steward of their education, he felt it would not be complete without having witnessed their government in action. *"Your political leaders work for you. You should know what they are doing, and why."*

So every year, right after graduation, seniors loaded onto a county bus and made the trip to visit the governor, see the legislature, and complete their rite of passage to adulthood. This year would be no different. Here, tradition still mattered.

"Okay, everybody, now that we've finished practice, we need to talk about the trip to Little Rock. As you know, it will only be a one-day event. And in order to accomplish that, we will leave the school grounds at exactly 6 a.m. and everyone needs to be on time. I have two parents that have volunteered to accompany us, but I'd prefer to have at least two more. If any of you have parents that can attend, please see me after this meeting, or have them call me tomorrow."

"Please dress according to the location that we're visiting and the weather. No halter tops or mini-skirts for girls, and you boys need to make sure you have on a nice button-up shirt. Remember, we are go-ing to the capital to meet the governor, not the Beatles. Does anyone have any questions?"

Gina sat in one of the chairs on the front row. It was hot in the auditorium, and she was exhausted from practice. *No, everybody wants to leave. No questions. I just wanna go home.*

Jo didn't really need to practice her speech again, but since she had the afternoon free, she thought she'd give it one more run.

They parted company around 2:30 and each girl headed home. Graduation was upon them, and the hard fact that life was changing crept into their thoughts. They needed time to think and reflect. Alone.

As Gina pulled into the drive, her dad stood in the doorway. He had a letter in his hand. Her heart sank. Not today. Not now.

The Felsenthal Letter

Jo turned onto the dirt road that led to her house, and stopped by the mailbox, just in case. She had begun losing hope that any kind of letter was coming.

I think they're just gonna ignore our applications, like we didn't even apply. Or maybe they won't bother to send a rejection notice. Surely, I'll get something before graduation. I've got to make some decisions if I can't go to the academy.

As she lowered the door on the mailbox, "USAF" stood out plainly in bold lettering on the return address of the envelope. Her name printed rigidly on the addressee line.

Oh my God. It's the letter. It's here. Oh my God.

She jumped back in the old Fairlane and floored it. She had to get home. She couldn't open it, not yet. She needed to be at home. Safe inside her house, in case the answer was no. If it was, she was going to break down, and she didn't want to do it out here.

"Momma, Momma, the letter... it's here! Where's Daddy? Still at work? Call him. Tell him it's here. See if he can come home. I'm so excited. I want him to be here when I open it. Call him, please."

"Hang on, Jo. He's already on his way home. I saw the letter earlier when I checked the mail, but I left it for you. I've already called him. He's coming now."

Jo had never been so excited and nervous in all her life.

Now I know how Robert felt a couple of weeks ago. That's why he made that God-awful yelping sound. He couldn't help it. He was about to explode.

It seemed forever before her Daddy pulled up in the truck. It took him only seconds to get in the house.

"Okay, sweetheart, open it. Let's see what the USAF thinks about my baby girl."

With that, she slid the kitchen knife along the side of the envelope, pulled out the letter, and unfolded the page. It was only one sheet of paper.

There, typed right underneath the Registrar of the Air Force Academy information she read: **LETTER OF ACCEPTANCE**

Jo's heartbeat pounded in her head. There was a buzzing sound in her ears. She was so excited, so overwhelmed. It was almost too much. The last few weeks of her life had been so turbulent, so emotional. And finally the letter had arrived.

Tears filled her momma's eyes as she smiled, so proud of her daughter. Her daddy, just as emotional but unwilling to openly cry, simply pulled his daughter close and hugged her with all the love he could muster.

After several minutes of tears, hugs, and celebration, Jo stopped to think of Gina. *I bet she got her letter, too.*

"Daddy, what about Gina? I wonder if she got her letter."

The Ingram Letter

"Gina, Gina, it's here! The letter! It's here!"

Her dad looked as if he were going to leap from the porch in order to get to her as she got out of the car.

"Okay, I see it. Give me a sec to get in the house."

Her heart hammered; she had no idea what she was going to do if it said "rejected" and even less if it said "accepted".

"Open it for me, Dad. I don't think I can do it."

That was the only invitation he needed. He slid the blade of his pocketknife down the side of the envelope. Slowly, he pulled the page from inside. It might as well have been cast in gold, for the painstaking care he took in removing it. Then, just as slowly, he opened the letter itself.

He never looked at the body of the letter. He simply saw "LETTER OF REJECTION" emblazoned in big black letters across the top of the page.

"I'm sorry, baby" his voice cracking, as he handed her the letter.

Gina began to read, aloud at first, and then as the tears began to fall, her voice broke. She couldn't finish reading aloud the horrible words that leapt at her from the page.

Jo and her mom and dad climbed into his pickup to make the short drive over to Gina's. She was still trembling with excitement, and couldn't wait to share the news with Gina. There was a chance Gina had been rejected, but it wasn't like she really cared, anyway. She would be so excited for Jo, regardless of the news her letter brought, if she had even gotten her letter yet.

Tom wanted to talk to Floyd, at any rate. He wasn't retired

military, and he had questions concerning the next steps now that Jo had received her letter.

Maureen came simply because she loved her daughter.

The drive over to Gina's was a short fifteen minutes, and Jo pinched herself the whole way. *This is truly happening.*

She bounced from the truck, racing across the yard to the front door. It took only seconds after reaching the kitchen, however, to realize that something was terribly wrong. Terribly, terribly wrong.

CHAPTER 6

Life is a Winding Road...filled with curves, and unexpected obstacles; deep valleys and breathtaking mountaintops. It's never an easy ride and we're never prepared. It's a love affair with the scenery that makes it a magnificent journey.

Louise Ingram, 1976

1976, Gina's Tomorrow's

GINA WOULD NEVER FORGET the moment she opened that letter. It was as if a hole had opened up and swallowed the young girl, full of fun and laughter, and a new person emerged: petrified and solemn.

I'm pregnant. No, no, I can't be. This isn't happening.

She had no idea how to deal with a baby, and no way to provide for one. With those thoughts came the image of Robert, and the knowledge that she must explain this to him. But first, she was going to have to explain to the two people standing in front of her. The two people that she loved so much and didn't want to disappoint. *Oh my God, this is going to hurt them so much.*

Gina raised her head from the letter to face her parents. They stood with questioning looks, waiting for her to read the rest of the letter. They were both so puzzled at her outpouring of tears, she hadn't after all, really wanted to go.

"I have to read the rest of this to you," she said, her voice a mere whisper.

She lowered her eyes once more to read the words written immediately following the big "REJECTION" statement.

Tears blurred her vision, not that she needed to see clearly, the information was already forever imprinted in her mind. But she would rather look at the paper than at her mom and dad's faces. She cleared her throat and began again.

Registrar, United States Air Force Academy

Colorado Springs, CO.

LETTER OF REJECTION

Ms. Ingram, we are sorry to inform you that your application for admission to the United States Air Force Academy could not be accepted.

As you are aware, one of the eligibility requirements mandates that you be unmarried with no dependents.

Based upon that fact, and the results of your medical examination, you do not meet basic eligibility requirements.

We do not at this time offer accommodations for children of Academy Officers.

Please contact your liaison officer, Lt. Col. John Listermann with any further questions.

When she finished reading, tears began anew, and she looked up at her parents. Her mom stood still in shock. She wasn't crying, she wasn't moving; she simply stood there. Her dad, however, looked crushed, his face ashen and haggard. His usually twinkling eyes and youthful smile, gone. His disbelief in the words his daughter read evident. Not Gina, not his baby.

At that very moment, Jo burst into the kitchen, excitement

bubbling over, until she had time to take in the scene before her. She stopped in mid-sentence at "Gina, I go…"

"What's happened? What's wrong? Why are you crying?"

Tom and Maureen stopped at the kitchen door.

Gina turned to look at her best friend. Her comrade in conspiracy, her hiking buddy, the girl she had come to love as if she were a sister, and a new round of emotions overtook her.

Somehow, amidst the racking sobs Gina managed to get out the word "pregnant."

Jo had simply stood in stunned silence. *Pregnant? Gina? How did you let this happen? What will we do?*

"You're pregnant? You're gonna have a baby?"

Jo's mom and dad had the foresight to excuse themselves, and only Jo remained.

The girls had spent so much time with each other, as well as with their families, that Floyd and Louise simply considered Jo one of their own. The following conversation must be shared with her as well.

The tears, from everyone in the house, flowed freely. Finally, after an hour or so, Jo finally pulled herself together enough to think of Robert. The moments of brief sentences and overwhelming sadness and disappointment for Floyd and Louise subsided into silence. Stark fear still gripped Gina.

"Gina," she had almost whispered, "you've got to find Robert."

Sobs, borne of despair, racked Gina this time. How can I tell him this, how can we deal with this if he goes to college? Can he still go to college?

Floyd interrupted her thoughts.

"Gina, you're gonna have to find Robert and share this news with him by yourself. You don't need me or your mom, this is something that should be shared between adults. If Robert is half the young man I believe him to be, you two will work this out."

At that, he took her mom and they went into the living room. The whole experience and revelation left them exhausted, and they needed time to absorb all that it meant to them, as parents and as a family.

"Do you want me to go with you, to tell him?"

"No, I didn't need you when it happened, Jo. I shouldn't need somebody now. I need to be alone with him to tell him. This is going to be the hardest thing I've ever done. It's gonna kill him." And the tears began to flow again

Although baseball season for spring had ended, Coach Fleming was spending extra time in the afternoon working with Robert. He wanted to make sure he was as ready and prepared as possible to attend the summer camp for South Arkansas University's baseball program. He was scheduled to leave the 21st of June for summer training, and to enroll as a student in their summer prep classes for new scholarship recipients.

As Gina pulled up at the field, she saw them coming off, laughing and talking together. She almost started to cry again. *Hold it together, girl, at least 'til Coach Fleming is gone.* It was pretty obvious that she had been crying. *Please let him leave quick and not wanna talk.*

She looked down at her lap, at her stomach, unable to see visible evidence of the life that was growing inside. She noticed her hands, and the ring he'd given her just a few short months ago. She thought of his class ring: *Today's dreams are tomorrow's future, but only if you make the right choices...*

"Hi, Gina. Robert and I are finished. I gotta go lock the gym. Congratulations, Miss Graduate. I'll see you Friday night."

"Thanks, Coach. Yessir. See ya Friday night." That was the most that she managed to muster.

Robert hopped in the car, opposite Gina.

"What's wrong, baby? Did you get that damn letter?"

"Yes, I did."

"Honey, it's alright. It doesn't matter if you didn't get accepted. To be honest, I'm kinda glad you didn't… I'd rather see if you can go with me…"

Gina started to cry again.

"That's not why I'm so messed up, Robert." Tears began flowing freely. She handed him the letter.

"It's because I'm pregnant."

There was a silence between them, a long deafening silence, she once again overcome with fear, fear that consumed her. *What if he…?*

"We have to get married, baby. We don't have any other choice. If I'm gonna have a baby, I'm gonna be around to be a daddy." His tone flat. Defeat evident on every inch of his face. One moment of passion, one single choice; that's all it took to eliminate every one of the others.

Robert's family would never be able to help support them if he went to college. They still had nine kids to finish raising. Floyd and Louise could help, but her dad had made it very clear that she had made an adult decision, and her life was now hers to lead.

She would never forget Robert's face in that moment of truth. He looked as if a giant weight had crushed his spirit as if the bottom fell out of his world. In that one, single second of her confession, college became a vanished dream. No baseball, no ticket out. He also realized that starting life with a baby was a huge responsibility, emotionally and financially.

Gina would also never forget the handsome young man that stood beside her throughout the process of giving the news to family and friends. Whatever kind of life she might have with Robert Phillips, it would be the best she could possibly make it.

The hardest part had been telling Robert, and the next would be going to church on Sunday. Everybody would be there: Jo and her mom and dad, Robert and his mom and dad; they would all be there and know. Not only was she scared and confused, she was coping with the embarrassment. The people at church loved her, but she also knew that they wouldn't approve of the situation.

Graduation and the next few days following were a blur for Gina. Just coming to grips with the fact that she discovered she would be a mother, lose Jo, and marry Robert, in the span of a day, was enough to fracture and blur the events of the next few days.

She spent many of those hours in tears and numbness. What would they do? How would they live? What would she do without Jo to talk to? These thoughts and questions, and many more, swirled inside Gina's head, as she and Robert made plans to marry. Of course, Robert Phillips, from strength of character and Ozark values would marry Gina. As he so solemnly put it, "We'll simply make the best of it, together."

Brother Timms from the church married them on June 5th at Gina's parents' home, with only the immediate family present. This, of course, included Jo and her parents. It was a simple ceremony, but one of the most remembered moments of Gina's life. Even now as she looked back, it was simply beautiful.

Robert was handsome, kind, and deeply in love with her, and it seemed the circumstances only brought them closer, both as friends and as a young couple. They moved into a rented house on Cedar Street, only a few miles from Gina's parents.

Robert's parents lived further out of town, almost a twenty-minute drive from the heart of Polk Ridge. Robert, however, willingly made the adjustment from farm life to a cramped two-bedroom house in town. They moved in the day he was supposed to report to summer practice at South Arkansas. His dad got him a job at the sawmill, and they readied themselves, and their little house, for a new baby.

She was twelve weeks into her pregnancy when she got the letter from the Air Force Academy, and it wasn't long after the wedding that morning sickness overtook her. She had a violent reaction to the heat, the smell of bacon, and even perfume for the next six months. She had never been so sick in all her life, or as lonely.

Jo left Little Rock at 10 a.m June 26th to report to USAF Academy in Colorado Springs. Everyone went to see her off, and as she boarded the plane, she turned to smile one last time at Gina. *What am I gonna do without her?* She smiled and waved back, hoping she couldn't see how desolate she felt.

With Jo gone, Robert working steadily, and the responsibilities of setting up and maintaining a household, she often felt overwhelmed and lost. She would never forget those first few months of loneliness and sadness.

She vowed to never let life catch her so unprepared and uncertain again. And as surely as the sun rises, and life continues, she lived to recall that promise several times over. She eventually realized that life will always be hard, some situations harder than others; it's how you cope that determines the journey and the ending.

She finally finished the Christmas decorations in the living room when she felt the first pangs and twinges of discomfort. It was only 1 o'clock, and it was Friday, Robert would be late. Today was a twelve-hour workday for him, and that meant he wouldn't even leave the mill until 7.

She went to the kitchen to call her mom. Her mom had been her rock since the pregnancy, the marriage and the lost scholarship had rocked her life. It was her mom that filled the emptiness for her when she needed a friend or to bend someone's ear as she learned to be a wife and mother.

Louise had been devastated when she learned that Gina was pregnant, but she dealt with the news in the same manner as she had most every other challenge in her life. She rolled up her sleeves and decided to make the best of it. She helped Robert and Gina find a house, helped Gina make it a home and given her all the advice and emotional support that she possibly could.

As an only child, Gina knew nothing when it came to babies and it was her mom that she turned to again and again. As the labor pains began, it was her mom she called. She had no idea how to determine if she needed to be at the hospital or if it was simply a false alarm. There was no sense in worrying Robert at work if it wasn't the real thing. She dialed the number.

William Jackson Phillips arrived three days before Christmas. The pregnancy, although full of morning sickness, had otherwise been an exceptionally uneventful experience for her. The minute "Jax" entered the world she fell in love twice over again. Robert remarked that his son had already bested him; he was an even better present than last year's class ring.

As teenage parents, they weren't prepared for the tremendous change the new baby brought to their household. Gina would later realize that no one is ever prepared for the changes that a baby brings.

Jax wasn't a sleeper, and not a quiet baby either; many long and sleepless nights were spent in the Phillips' home those first few months and she marvelled how something so small made so much noise! Her days were filled with meeting the needs of a baby, cooking and cleaning, and missing her friend.

She longed to talk to Jo. There was so much that she wanted to tell her, ask her, or just have a good laugh or cry, depending on the day's events. But the only way to reach her was by phone at a designated time and place. And Jo was immersed in her own life, many miles and circumstances apart.

Robert and Gina added another member to their household only a couple of years after Jax. A beautiful tiny little girl, who turned out to be the complete opposite of her loud, sleepless brother.

The pregnancy, although lacking morning sickness, had been

hard on her and when Millicent Marie Phillips finally arrived, she decided she needed no more. Thankfully, Robert felt the same way.

Jax and Millie were a mixture of Robert and Gina in the most comical of ways. Jax, although an almost perfect replica of his dad in stature and looks, had her personality, always full of mischief and humor. Millie, on the other hand, had her momma's looks and build, but was as shy in nature as her daddy. Amazing how such a disastrous start could produce such wonderful little blessings.

As she watched her children play, she often stopped to reflect on the differences in childhood from one generation to the next. *They would've loved Jo. Their childhoods are so much alike.*

They began and graduated school in Polk Ridge, living each day in much the same way that Jo had, knowing only the Ozarks as home.

Gina and Robert spent their days raising their children, working hard to provide, and filling up their weekends with family and music, thanks to the Phillips clan. Jax and Millie had more than enough family to surround them, thanks to Tom and Maureen, who looked upon Gina as an adopted member of their family. Jax and Millie always referred to them as Uncle Tom and Aunt Maureen.

It would be from Maureen that she heard the latest news about Jo: where she was, what she was doing. She tried in the first few years to stay in contact with her, and Jo had returned the effort. There had been several letters in the first few months apart and a few phone calls. Slowly as time and each woman's life began to fill with differences the letters and phone calls became less frequent; there was less and less to share. By the time Jax started to school, they hadn't talked in over a year.

The first few years of life "after Jo" brought so many changes for Gina. A husband, children, and running a household, but for the most part, she was content, and happy with her life. The only black spot in the contentment: she wanted someone to talk to, someone like Jo. Robert simply wasn't interested in the places she had been or any of the things about life she and Jo shared. The ironic thing was that now many of those dreams and plans were mute. Her life was with Robert, and their conversations were centered around sawmills, sawmill problems, and raising children. She really missed Jo. Finally she realized it was just her friend she missed.

CHAPTER 7

THAT SEPTEMBER MORNING STARTED off as an ordinary day. Gina cooked breakfast for Robert, kissed him goodbye, and then got her children ready for the day: breakfast, school for Jax, and errands and chores for her and Millie.

She and Robert had a "slight difference of opinion" (as her mom often chose to refer to marital discord) that morning as they ate breakfast. She gave in and then wondered why she ever argued with Robert. Marriage was a definite process of compromise—mostly filled with her compromises, too.

"Gina, when Jax gets home this afternoon, you're gonna have to help him with his homework. I'm not gonna get off 'til at least 7, and he needs to be finished with it and ready for bed by 8."

"Robert, he's not gonna want me to help him, we always struggle when I help him…"

"I know, but I won't have time to do it tonight. Simply tell him he has no choice. I know what's wrong; it's because you don't wanna look at those school books. But Gina, I won't be home in time. You gotta help him."

"I can't drop everything at that time of day and sit down to do homework. I've got supper to get ready, laundry to finish, and Millie won't be still long enough for me to help Jax."

"Yes, she will. Just give her something to play with. Give her that book I brought home from work the other day. It won't matter if she writes on it, or colors it; that'll keep her busy while you help Jax. We don't have a choice today, Gina."

The resolute tone in his voice told her there wouldn't' be anything to discuss further. She sighed.

Yes, marriage required constant compromise.

She decided as soon as she finished her morning's errands to give her mom a call as she made lunch for Robert. Because they lived in town, the mill was only a six-minute drive from their house. It was convenient for Robert to go to work and come home for lunch. But that also meant fixing lunch and supper for a man with a big appetite.

Surely after talking to her mom, she would find a way to bridge their morning's differences. Millie would be ready to take a nap soon, and there might be a few quiet minutes to herself.

This is really something I've got to deal with; I have children, and I'm gonna have to help them with their schoolwork. I just wish it didn't bring back feelings of frustration and anger. And I get upset with them… it's not fair. Talking it over with Mom will help.

With her day carefully planned, Gina ran errands and made time for a quick stop by the Krusty Kup. She enjoyed going by the diner for coffee and an opportunity to catch the latest gossip.

The Krusty Kup was on the corner of the courthouse square. It was the social gathering place for Polk Ridge and was often filled to capacity when court was in session. Most of the buildings that surrounded the courthouse were as old as the courthouse itself, and the Krusty Kup was no different. The renovated windows of the Krusty Kup were enlarged. They were now solid sheets of glass, allowing patrons to view the square's activity as they munched on food or simply gathered for a morning cup of coffee.

The inside of the restaurant was filled with the sounds and smells of conversation, cooks and waitresses completing orders, and the smell of coffee and delicious food. Breakfast was served throughout the day, but from 10 a.m. to 2 p.m., there was fried chicken, steak with gravy, and a smorgasbord of garden vegetables.

Gina never missed an opportunity to gather with other townspeople. She loved the food and the conversation there. It was always a welcome change from the solitary existence of a housewife and mother.

After her morning stop by the Krusty Kup, she pulled into the driveway a few minutes before 10 a.m., with a sleepy Millie and lunch on her mind. She carried the sleeping little girl in the house and laid her on the couch. As she headed out the front door to retrieve the bags from the morning's shopping, Robert pulled in.

Why's he home so early? Wonder if something happened at work. Surely he didn't get laid off, or worse—fired.

The early '80's were not a prosperous time for many sawmills, especially one in Polk Ridge.

He never left early or missed work. He was as steady as the morning sunrise, and Gina always gave thanks to her Maker for the blessing that Robert was to her life, even when they disagreed.

He never got out of the truck but called out to her.

"Gina, you need to come quick. There's something wrong with your momma."

"What's wrong with her? I've got Millie asleep on the couch. What do I need to do?"

"You get your purse. I'll get Millie. We need to get over there."

He didn't tell her the whole truth. There was no need to say anything until he found out exactly what happened. Floyd had been nearly incoherent when he called. Robert told him to just hang up and go see about Louise. Before he left, though, he asked the lady in the guard shack to call the ambulance and gave her the address to their home.

Once again, Gina faced a blurred recollection of events. She scarcely remembered getting into the truck with Robert or arriving at her parent's home.

She would, however, forever recall the sight of her mother lying on the living room couch. She lay peacefully in death. She would also never forget the sobs of her father for the loss of his wife. Her mother suffered a massive stroke, a cerebral aneurysm, sometime during mid-morning. When Floyd returned from his trip to town, he found her lying just as she was now, already gone. Gina remembered the look of desolation and grief that consumed her dad. He seemed to grow much older at that moment. His shoulders were hunched in defeat, his eyes hollow and face drawn.

The arrangements and events of the following days left Gina once again bereft, in a sea of confusion. She had now lost two of the most important people in her life. Women that had shaped and formed her early years, her mom to death and Jo to the military.

Jo wasn't able to come home for the funeral, but thanks to Maureen, Gina managed to cope. It took weeks, though, before her grief finally subsided and she began to sleep at night without waking up to tears. Tears and remorse for not calling her mother before she ran errands that day.

I should've taken five minutes to call her before I went to town. I had no idea it was gonna be my last chance to say "I love you."

She learned another valuable lesson that colored her actions for years: *Seize the moment.* Never let the opportunity to tell someone how you feel pass by. It may never come again.

It was almost a year to the day of her mom's passing that her dad called her and asked what they were doing later that afternoon. She could still clearly remember the conversation.

"Hey, sweetheart. What y'all got planned for supper? Is Robert working late, or will he be home around 5:30 tonight? I wanted to come by and visit a little while."

"Sure, Dad. We're here at home. No, Robert's not working late tonight –not until Thursday or Friday. I'm fixin' fried chicken, creamed potatoes, peas and fried okra. Why don't you come on over around 5 p.m. and we can visit before we eat?"

"Sounds good. See ya then, sweetheart."

He visited with them on a regular basis, primarily because he was lonely. He could've gone down to the Moon Café or the Krusty Kup if he only wanted to eat. He wanted his family's company.

She could tell that her dad was lonely since her mom died. His hair had grayed so much within a year, and wrinkles of worry and pain creased every part of his face. She hadn't, however, realized how alone he might feel in their house, surrounded by the many things her mom collected over the years. She was an avid collector. It was her hobby: bowls, bells, books, and coffee cups. Those were her specialties. Everywhere he looked, he was reminded of her. The only thing that he sincerely relished looking at were the scrapbooks she'd put together when they traveled across Europe.

She'd started the first one in Germany right before Gina was born, and a new scrapbook was made for every airbase. When they reached Polk Ridge, she began to put them together according to every major life event: one for their new home, one for Gina's first year at school in Polk Ridge, and one for her days spent cheering. She knew Gina would rather look at pictures than read a story.

"Gina! Where you at?" Floyd shouted.

She heard him call from the front yard.

"In the back, Dad. I decided to grill tonight since you were coming. Thought you might want a steak rather than fried chicken."

"Where's Robert?"

"He's coming. He got off at 5 p.m., so he'll be here in just a few. You want something to drink. Sweet tea, maybe?"

"No, I'll wait on him to get home. I thought we might share a beer together. I don't have much time with my son-in-lay. I don't think it can be easy livin' with you and those grandkids!" His eyes twinkled, and he laughed. "Remember, I spent eighteen years raising you!"

At that moment Robert rounded the corner. He'd heard them talking as he crossed the yard.

"Mr. Floyd!" The two embraced. "Glad you could come over. It gives Gina something to talk about other than my day. God knows I don't really want to re-live that!" And he laughed; he had such an easy laugh, one that made everyone else want to share in the good feeling.

If Robert ever resented anything about their life and the opportunity that had been snatched away from him, he never even hinted at it to Gina. In fact, he never talked about that day. On the few occasions Gina tried, he had resolutely closed the door on that topic. The only thing he ever said when it came to the lost chance was when she told him she was pregnant:

"We both made a choice, Gina, and we were well aware of the consequences of that choice."

I suppose not talking about it is his way of protecting me from his real thoughts. If you never talk about it, you can't say anything hurtful.

Floyd sat down in a chair that surrounded the grill and picnic table in their backyard.

"Sit down, you two. I need to talk to you."

He had a proposal and wanted to approach them together because he felt this was a decision they needed to make together. After spending the last few months alone in the house he and Louise built together, and everything in it reminding him of her, he wanted to make a change..

It was time to do something different. He wanted them to move into the home where he and Louise had shared memories and Gina spent her adolescent years. They built the house without a mortgage, and at this point, he wanted to simply give them the house.

It would be a little further for Robert to drive to work, but not by much. Jax and Millie would have their own room. And as he pointed out, it was where Gina vanished for hours on end into the woods of the Ozarks and experienced endless adventures. He wanted to move into town and rent the house they were in. Although he didn't say it, Gina guessed he wanted the closeness that town and townspeople would provide for him.

As they listened and talked with Floyd, they began to love his proposal. The paid-for house would be less expensive compared to renting the house on Cedar Street, and more room was a welcome change for their young, growing family. Robert was especially happy because the house was closer to his parents, and the house was more like the home he had known as a child. So Gina moved back home.

When they moved in, her dad didn't want to take many things with him. He left her every scrapbook and most of the furniture. The collections of bells, books, and coffee cups remained in the cupboards or shelves where they had been when her mom passed. *They can be sorted through later*, she decided. There would be plenty of time in years to come; no need to rush. She half-heartedly thought that her dad might change his mind once he got himself situated in the house in town; he might later want some of the things he was so willing to leave behind now.

Jax and Millie grew into young adolescents in the same rooms that Gina had occupied as she turned from a young teen into a young woman. The house was filled with activity once again, and on more than one occasion, Gina pondered how her mother made this look so easy.

Jax was the natural athlete his father had been. As soon as he was eligible for junior varsity football and baseball, Gina spent many afternoons back and forth between home and a sports field. If she wasn't at the field watching him practice, she watched him with his dad in the backyard. One Saturday morning when Jax was a freshman, Robert took him to the backyard to practice his swing.

It was hot, and Gina saw the perspiration on their clothes from the kitchen window. She was headed out the back door to ask them if they wanted some sweet tea when she realized they were sitting on the back steps. Father and son lost in conversation. She didn't want to eavesdrop, but the subject of the conversation stopped her in her tracks.

"Dad, you're really pretty good at baseball, and you're a good teacher. You understand so much why didn't you become a coach or go to college?"

"Well, son, that's a pretty tough question to answer. I think since you're fifteen years old and starting high school, it's a good idea for me to be honest with you. I need to tell you why I didn't go to college. When I was seventeen, I made some choices that had consequences. One of those consequences made it impossible for me to go to college even though I had a baseball scholarship."

"You had a scholarship? To where?"

"South Arkansas University, as a freshman starter. I guess I was pretty good." He smiled at Jax. "But pretty good didn't matter. You see, Jax, when you're a young man, it's hard to look ahead and see what might happen tomorrow. You have to realize that actions have conequences. Sometimes those consequences are hard. Especially when you don't give enough thought to something you do. Your mom and I were already in love then, just as we are today. We made a choice, and as a result, you came along. When we found out that you were coming, I couldn't play baseball at college, not when I needed to be a dad. And so here we are today. I've got a star athlete right here at home, though, and one that has the opportunity to go play baseball at college, which is something I didn't do."

Jax sat for a minute in contemplation; thinking and mulling over what his dad had shared.

"So, you don't want me to blow a scholarship, right?"

"Right, son. I am counting on you to do some of the things I didn't. Go to college, get an education, and make a better way for the family you might have someday."

Gina was moved to tears. Only her husband would be able to find a way to turn something that had been so hard into something so special. She moved away from the screen door, not wanting to interrupt the moment between them. She heard Millie calling for her, and the moment of reflection was lost.

Millie reminded Gina more of Jo than herself. The girl kept her nose in a book and was at the top of her class at school. The one stark difference was her shy nature. She had no idea where the shy bone came from. Although Robert had been somewhat shy in high school, it wasn't as bad as the almost hermit-like behavior that Millie exhibited. Nothing seemed to bring her out of her shell. As she got older, it only seemed to get worse.

"C'mon, Millie," Gina would ask, "Surely you've managed to find at least one girlfriend at school?"

But she continued to be quite the loner. She did, however, have a deep love of the Ozark Mountains, and disappeared just as Gina had for hours into the woods surrounding the house. Quite often she asked her daughter just how she spent her time absent from the house, and Millie would only reply that she was "observing nature." *Yes,* Gina thought, *she is a different child.*

And so the years rolled by with each child growing into young adults and Gina finding happiness and comfort in her family circle.

During Jax's freshman year, she suffered yet another loss of family; only this time it wasn't quite as close to home as her mother's death had been.

It was on a Thursday afternoon, and she would never forget the phone call.

"Gina?" Maureen's faltering voice on the other end, gave her cause for alarm.

"Yes, ma'am, it's me. What's wrong?"

"I'm at the hospital in Flowood. It's Tom. Something's really wrong. I brought him from the co-op. I need to get ahold of Stella bad, but he's in ICU, and they don't have a phone except in the waitin' room. Can you call her, honey, and tell her to come quick? I tried to call her before I called you, but she's not answering the phone, and I hate those messaging machines."

"Yes, ma'am, I can. I'll be glad too. Can I do anything for you? Do you need me to come?"

"No, honey, not yet. He just couldn't talk and was real fuzzy about everything when I got to the co-op, and it just got worse on the way over here. I just don't have an answer yet. And Gina, thanks… but just wait about coming 'til we find out what's wrong. I may need you more when we get home."

"Well, okay. I'll get Stella. Oh, wait, Miss Maureen, what's the number there? In case Stella wants to call you back, or I need to get you?"

Maureen gave her the number, and Gina spent the next few hours contacting Stella and alerting her dad. The three of them were closer than ever since Louise passed, and Gina wanted to tell him herself.

Tom had suffered a fate almost identical to Louise, except for the fact that he managed to linger long enough for Jo to return home. She was stationed in Japan at the time, and it took her two long days to make it back to her father's side. Gina finally had the opportunity to visit with Jo, but it was under circumstances that didn't afford the girls a real heartfelt reunion.

The funeral home was already packed when Gina arrived. As she pulled up, she could see the line of visitors was already spilling into the parking lot.

Mr. Tom knew everybody. What a crowd. Poor Jo, Stella, and Miss Maureen. They'll be exhausted. Maybe I can spend a little time with Jo...

Finally, a half hour later, Gina reached the inside of the room. She saw Jo, Stella, and Jack, and Miss Maureen at the casket. There were still people everywhere, and the walls were lined with flowers and green plants.

Yes, Mr. Tom had plenty of people payin' their respects. I wish Robert could have come to the viewing. I really don't want to be here alone. Jo looks good, circumstances considered. She looks so professional, so regal in that uniform. I hope we can talk for just a minute.

Finally, Gina reached them. Miss Maureen was pale and shaken. It was obvious the doctor had given her something; she just didn't seem like herself. Jo, on the other hand, seemed calm in an almost surreal way.

She isn't crying. I was a wreck when Momma died. Maybe she took something, too. It's been so long since I saw her. I wouldn't know if she had anyway.

"Hey, Jo, Miss Maureen. I'm so sorry. I loved Mr. Tom so much."

"Gina, honey, thank you for coming. I just don't know what I'm gonna do without him. I just ain't prepared for this. Not yet." Tears began to flow again.

It was Jo's turn to speak.

"Hi, Gina. Thanks for coming. It means so much to me and Momma that you came. Where's Robert?"

"He's still working. Sometimes he's late gettin' off, and today was one of those days. He said to tell you he's very sorry for your loss. He's comin' to the funeral tomorrow. Miss Maureen, is there anything I can do to help you? Do you need me or Robert to do anything at the house? I guess you've probably had company and folks bringing food, but do you need anything else?"

"No, sweetheart. Jo and Stella are taking care of everything at the house. No, there's nothing for anybody to do. Not now."

During the course of her conversation with Maureen, Jo had turned her attention to the next person in line, and the opportunity for further conversation was lost.

Jo could only stay long enough for the funeral, and then it was back to Japan and back to her career.

After Tom's passing, it was Gina who made sure that Maureen had time to heal with people she loved. Stella lived almost fifty miles from Polk Ridge, and with the three children she was raising, rarely had free time to visit with her mom. Having already lost her own mother, Gina was more than happy to comfort Maureen.

They had similar personalities and spent a great deal of free time together. They enjoyed the gossip of the Krusty Kup, Jax's games, and weekend BBQ's while Robert entertained them with the fiddle. Maureen spoke of Jo often, and provided Gina with her latest assignment, transfer, and travels, but Gina felt as if she was talking about a different person. Their lives had lost their common thread.

Maureen and Floyd were good company for each other, especially since widowhood can be such a lonely place. They watched with Gina and Robert as Jax grew into an excellent ball player, just like his dad, and Millie grew up.

Jax graduated with a baseball scholarship to South Arkansas University. It was like watching history repeat itself. Unlike their situation, however, he enrolled without incident, and by the time Millie prepared to graduate, he was in his sophomore year, a successful ball player and finance major.

During his years at the sawmill, he had moved from hourly hand to night shift manager, and then to day shift manager, and finally, general manager. She was ever aware of the blessing she'd received in Robert Phillips.

And as they lived, day by day, he kept his promise to make the best of their life together. And she worked just as hard to support him in every way possible. As his job became his career, and as their children grew, she took care of everything when it came to the running of their household. If he worked late, she made sure things at home ran like clockwork. From bills, to groceries, to meals, she tried very hard to never let her husband down. They had beaten the odds for young married couples that even under the best of circumstances can experience failure.

At thirty-seven, Gina had experienced so many life trials: pregnant and married at eighteen, losing her mother when she was only twenty-four and Tom only a few years after that. She had raised two children and had a life filled with the ups and downs of raising children in a small town in the Ozarks. She was no stranger to hard work and loss. As she approached her fortieth birthday, her thoughts turned often to Jo. How was her life?

Now that things are slowing down and the kids are almost grown, I really need to try to contact her. There must be something left of the friendship we shared even if our lives are completely different now.

There just never seemed to be those few minutes she needed to give her a call or send a letter.

As spring of 1996 arrived in the Ozarks, Millie was ready to graduate. Millie, the "bookworm" and "nature child" as Gina lovingly referred to her as, was graduating from school in May. As salutatorian, she had secured a scholarship to Mississippi State University in the agricultural program. Her "observation of nature" turned out to be her calling in education and life. MSU had a great agricultural program that included an undergraduate degree in natural resources and environmental management. This was Millie's first choice in careers.

She wanted to return to the Ozarks to focus on their beauty as a natural resource. She wanted to contribute to their continued preservation through environmental management with the National Park system.

Gina marveled at her wonderful, talented children. She was a very proud parent and thankful that she and Robert gave them a good start in life.

Her mom had given her one small piece of advice when she and Robert married. Years later, she was so thankful that she had listened to her mother. She told her to make scrapbooks to remember every moment:

Gina, honey, you have no idea what a comfort those old pictures and clippings will be one day. It's the link between the present and past, a way to revisit wonderful moments that are gone and only remain in bits and pieces in your mind. Pictures help you recall and relive those precious times.

Now that both of them were grown, she had so many memories clipped and pasted together in books to cherish. She wished she had the opportunity to tell her mom how much wisdom there had been in that small piece of advice. How often she flipped through those pages and relived some of her proudest moments.

It was early in May and she looked out her kitchen window to one of the most beautiful sunrises she surely had ever seen.

"Mornin', baby. What's for breakfast today?" As he approached her from behind, he followed up his question with a kiss and a bear hug.

"I fixed you somethin' special today, especially since it's exactly one month today' til our anniversary."

"Is that your way of reminding me that we're celebrating twenty years of marriage? Do you realize we've been together *twenty* years? Where did so many years go?"

She sighed. She didn't know. It seemed like only yesterday…

"To be honest, honey, I don't have a clue where those twenty years went. I can't imagine my life without you, the years have been so good to us. What do you suppose the next twenty will bring? Reckon you'll look as good then as you do today?" She turned from him to tend to the bacon on the stove.

He continued to gaze at his wife. She was the one that was still just as beautiful today as she'd been that Christmas Eve so long ago when he'd given her the ring.

They finished breakfast together, and she watched him stride effortlessly to the truck and thought to herself that at thirty-seven, he was still very much a man in his prime. He wasn't that tall, but he was square-shouldered, slim of waist, and with such a confident air--so much appeal. He was so sure of his place as a man. She sighed. Yes, she was a lucky woman.

I realize I'm not the only female that notices how attractive my husband is, and I guess I should be thankful he works in a sawmill. There's not that many women there, and I sure don't have to worry about his secretary. Carly's as good as gold, and I think she looks at Robert as more of a father than a boss.

He left every morning at 7:15 and every morning she then turned her attention to Millie and getting her youngest child off to school. Millie, as studious as she was, was never in a hurry to get anywhere.

As she fixed her daughter's breakfast, she once again revisited the thought she had been turning over in her mind that maybe the time had arrived for her to return to school. Time to open the door to her own career. The once self-professed hater of education finally saw at thirty-seven what she had not seen at seventeen: there was satisfaction and opportunity in a career and an education.

Millie finished her breakfast and drove off to school in the old Pontiac they had bought for her when she turned sixteen. It wasn't a new car, but it was reliable and would get her from Point A to Point

B, and that was their greatest concern. "Cool" never was a part of the equation for them, or for Millie.

Funny how it's so different for Millie than it was for me. I was so in love with the Mustang Momma and Daddy got for me. It was so important to be cool and fit in. Millie doesn't care.

The Mustang was sold the same summer Gina and Robert got married, the same summer she was pregnant. A housewife doesn't need a rag-top Mustang, and they needed the money. Those facts didn't keep her from crying when she watched it leave though. Losing the Mustang was just another reminder that her life had changed.

As she began her morning's work, the phone rang. She looked at the clock.

It's only 8:30. Maureen's calling early. I haven't even finished in the kitchen. She must want to go somewhere today.

"Hey," she began, thinking that her second mom was on the other end.

"Miss Gina, this is Carly." Her voice broke, and she began to cry.

"Mr. Robert… he's on his way to the hospital… there was an accident, and we called the ambulance, but I think you better get to Flowood pretty quick."

"What kind of accident?" she asked, suddenly finding it hard to breathe and think simultaneously.

"I don't know… I think it's pretty bad."

"Oh no, what…? Why…? Okay, I'll leave now," Gina mumbled and hung up. She had to call her dad. She had to…

She grabbed her purse and keys. *Forget it, I'll call 'em when I get there.*

There is one stark fact that every small town faces: the residents of these small towns are miles away from medical facility care. Yes, almost every small town has a doctor for colds and minor cuts and scrapes, but any real medical emergency is usually a thirty- minute trip to somewhere else. Flowood was a thirty-five minute trip from Polk Ridge.

Her thoughts ran rampant on the thirty-five minute drive to Flowood. She ran the gamut of possibilities: he might have lost his arm, his leg, crushed a hand; the possibilities were endless, and she was well aware of the dangers of working in a sawmill. She had already witnessed lost legs and arms, hands, and eyesight in the twenty years Robert had worked there. *Well, whatever's happened, we'll be alright. It won't be too devastating. The kids are grown and we can make it even if he's lost an arm or leg.*

Finally, she saw the blue hospital sign and the entrance to the emergency area. As she entered through the emergency doors, she tried to calm herself. *He doesn't need a hysterical wife, not right now.*

She searched for the information desk to try to determine where her husband had been taken, if there was surgery, and what she needed to do. Within just a few minutes of her arrival, she didn't even try to control her emotions, as they took her to the trauma room.

By the time she got to him, there wasn't much left of the rock that had been her husband. Blood was everywhere, and his face was ashen, as though death had already claimed him. The entire room was in disarray, doctors and nurses alike had worked on him and gauze, needles, and tubes were strewn around the room. Finally, as Gina arrived, they exhausted their options. Too much internal damage was done; nothing stopped the bleeding.

"Baby, I'm here." Sobs racked her body and took control of her voice.

"Robert, I'm here… can you hear me?" She watched the shallow rise and fall of his chest, or what was left of it. She could see the damage that had been done to his body and knew instinctively it wasn't going to be fixed.

"R'gina, so sorry… love you… so sorry…"

She didn't care where she was, who was there, or what needed to be done... Gina grasped his face in her hands, trying to make sure he saw her, could hear her...

Between the damage to his body, the loss of blood and the morphine, he was barely conscious.

"Robert, it's okay... it's okay, you're gonna be alright, the doctors..."

"No, doc can't fix... too much... wrong..."

"I love you too... it's okay... you'll be okay...don't go, Robert, don't leave me.... don't leave..." The last was more of a wailing shriek than spoken words. He never opened his eyes as he drew his last breath.

She lay as close as she could, sobbing and crying for what seemed like forever. She wasn't aware of time or space. Only Robert, only her wonderful husband....

After Carly called Gina, she called Floyd. As Robert's assistant, she had everyone's contact information, and Gina was going to need someone, some kind of family and kin. She already knew what she didn't say to Gina. The damage was too much, the emergency room too far.

Through her tears, Carly relayed to Floyd the morning's events, and it was through her dad that Gina would finally hear the recounting of the morning's events.

When Robert arrived at the mill, most of the sawmill's fifty or so hands had been at work since 6 a.m. and the day was in full swing. The first problem that confronted him as he arrived was the de-barker. When it malfunctioned, that led to a shutdown on the conveyor and feed to the saw, and it was downhill from there. Of course, when you have one piece of equipment to tear up, others are sure to follow.

Next there was the crane and then came the saw. The third issue proved to be the fatal one for Robert. Once he was caught between the logs and the saw, there was no good outcome for the man that had sacrificed himself, first for his family, and now for his work.

The ambulance arrived in less than ten minutes, but the thirty-five minute trip to the emergency room proved to be far too long.

Floyd and Millie arrived twenty minutes after Gina. He realized when he asked where he could find his son-in-law and the nurse dropped her eyes, that the news would be bad, really bad. He had been the one to tell Millie and to take a devastated Gina home.

Robert Phillips was laid to rest three days after the accident.

Once again, the blurring of days and events overtook Gina. This time, it would take every ounce of resolve she had, and the thought of her two children to help her cope with the enormity of Robert's death. She knew as a mother she had to struggle through the loss and devastation, to find a way to overcome. But as a woman and a wife, she alternated between anger, remorse, and the urge to simply give up. She'd never faced life so alone and so bereft.

Why did this happen? Why? I still need him so much. He took care of so many things. I don't even know where to begin. What about Jax and Millie? They still need their daddy. Why, Robert, why did you step down off that conveyor? It was too dangerous. Now, because of that one choice, he's gone. He's gone and I'm not ready to be a widow.

She thought of Jo, but never once considered reaching out to her old friend. Jo couldn't help her now; she didn't even feel any comfort at the thought of her.

Jax came home from college for the next two weeks, postponing his semester exams with the consent of the university to help his mother in any way he could. Millie never walked with her graduating class, and although she should have, she didn't leave her mother's side. Floyd and Maureen did everything they could to ease the loss for Gina, but couldn't manage to console her. Life was turned on its head, and she just couldn't manage to clear *her* head and cope with the fact that Robert was gone.

In the several weeks that followed, Gina spent most of her days and nights in tears. She was so unprepared, so uncertain as to how she should go on. Finally, Gina awoke one morning and looked in the mirror. The image that gazed back at her was a woman she didn't recognize. Her face was puffy, swollen from crying. Her hair a matted mess, she was pale with dark circles under her blue eyes that only served to enhance a ghastly appearance.

This is not what Robert would expect from the woman he loved, the woman that raised his children. He never faltered, he never wavered. No matter how great his burdens, no matter what happened, he shouldered the responsibility and moved on. Surely, you owe him that much, Gina. Get up, get up and take care of your responsibilities. She began to cry, but this time it was different. This time it was with the knowledge that she would survive, she would go on, whether she wanted to or not.

Jax had returned to school, and Millie was still at home because everyone was so worried about Gina. It was mid-July, Millie should have been making preparations to start the fall semester at MSU. Gina finally realized this fact as well. There were things to do, children to see about, and plans to make. She pulled herself together, rolled up her sleeves, and went to work.

The remainder of the summer was spent dealing with lawyers, enrolling Millie in college and getting her things transferred to MSU. Making sure that Jax had what he needed to return to his junior year of college, settling any outstanding issues from Robert's funeral, and putting their personal affairs in order.

She had run the household, but he had taken care of their financial obligations. Other than taking care of the electric bill, water bill, or groceries, she had no experience to draw upon when it came to the remaining financial decisions.

For this, she turned to an old friend and boss, Melvin Kroon. After his first two years with Dairy Queen, he'd been offered a new location. But when the time came to leave and move up the management ladder, he was reluctant to go. Choosing instead to buy a business of his own: The Krusty Kup. Melvin and The Krusty Kup became a favorite with the residents for two reasons: one, it was the only coffee shop and diner combination; and two, Melvin truly loved the Ozark townspeople, and they loved him.

He wasn't married, and for him, the folks of Polk Ridge were his family. For the last two decades, he had poured coffee, offered advice, and been a part of their small town. When he bought the Krusty Kup, he offered Gina a job, but she'd declined to go back to work, especially with small children at home. They had, however, remained friends throughout the years, and if anyone could help her now, it was Melvin.

Robert would want that too. Although he had often teased Gina about Melvin, and on more than one occasion proclaimed that the "painfully shy Melvin" was still waiting on her, he truly liked and respected Melvin.

Kind of ironic. Robert said on more than one occasion if anything happened to him, at least he knew Melvin would take care of me. I just don't think either one of us thought it would be like this. Oh, Robert… I still can't believe you left me…

She called Melvin late one afternoon when she thought the café traffic was slow and asked if she could have a minute of his time; she needed to talk with him. He made time that very afternoon.

"Hi, Melvin. How's everything at the Krusty Kup? I know I haven't been in much lately, I haven't been anywhere much, lately. These last few months have been pretty hard."

"Yeah, I know they have. Are you finally pulling things together? I know the loss was bad, Gina, but you'll survive, and you'll be alright."

"I know, I finally realized that. And for as bad as the loss was, dealing with the legal stuff is almost just as bad. That's why I wanted to talk to you."

"There's a lot to deal with, isn't there? You never realize how much you lean on somebody 'til they're gone."

She almost began to cry again. Just thinking of the fact that he was gone was enough to bring on the tears.

"Melvin, I don't know anything when it comes to estates, wills, or settlements, or even property tax. I've been dealing with the legal stuff the best I can, but I'm in over my head. I wanted to ask you if you would let me hire you to help me. I trust you. We've been friends for a long time, and you deal with business stuff all the time. Do you have time?"

"Nope. I'm not for hire, Gina."

She stared at him, disbelief apparent. She hadn't thought he would say no.

"I'm only available as a friend. Not to be paid. I'll be glad to help you, because I care about you, honey, not because I want any money."

From that moment forward, he was a constant support for Gina. Helping with financial decisions, giving advice and sharing his thoughts on the best thing to do, and soothing away tears at times. Although no one ever asked, and she never volunteered, most could see that their relationship became more than just "old friends."

It was Melvin that finally approached her about returning to school, pointing out that she was still very young. A career, a job, might be good for her. Emotionally and financially. She conceded that she'd been giving that idea some thought, even before the accident, but had no idea where to start. He did.

Melvin Kroon kept an ear to the ground about everything

happening in Polk Ridge and was an invaluable resource when it came to the latest news. He said there was federal aid available for social workers in most of the counties of Arkansas. Since they were mostly rural and lacked in public services for many of the poorest residents.

Polk County (for which Polk Ridge happened to be the county seat) was one of the poorest counties in Arkansas. The county commissioners were working on a proposal to build a social services facility offering mental health and drug counseling services. He suggested that Gina return to college and get her education in social work. She could complete her college courses, get her degree and apply for a position at the new facility just about the time the facility opened.

It would, he explained, take at least two years for the county commissioners to put their plan into action and build the facility. She gave some thought to Melvin's suggestion, and it soon began to make sense. She had lived here most of her life, she knew many of the residents, and this work would be something that could give her a purpose and personal satisfaction.

She started to school the fall of Jax's senior year of college, and Millie's sophomore year. Many times over the next years she laughed and commented that her whole house was in college at the same time! Who would have ever thought Gina Phillips was college material?

She enrolled and began classes the same fall that the county commissioners got the go ahead to build and staff the new facility: The North Arkansas Ozark Family Services Center. It didn't take Melvin long to inform the commissioners that he had just the perfect person to hire to help them get things up and going. It also didn't take Gina long to fully convince the commissioners that she really was the person for the job.

She gave college every ounce of the same dedication that she had given her husband and her family. The day she entered the doors, she knew this would take much more work than classes in high school had required all those years ago. The biggest obstacle she faced was coaxing those wheels of learning in her head to turn once again. It had been over twenty years since Gina had opened a textbook, and the learning didn't come as easy now as it had then. Not that it ever came easy for her.

The second problem: technology. There were new computers in the college classroom, and for her, it might as well have been the technology that landed the astronauts on the moon. She had not one clue how to operate a computer, let alone complete her work in a program such as WordPerfect, or Lotus, or the new spreadsheet software, Excel. On more than one occasion, Melvin coached her along, pushing her to continue, no matter how overwhelming the classroom seemed.

Jax and Millie were great help as well, and she would often turn to her son, just as she had his daddy, for help. It was Jax she telephoned when she simply couldn't understand some instruction she'd been given about a document or a formula. It was Jax that came home on more than one occasion to give personal instructions to a frustrated and disgusted Gina. Even with the torment and torture, late nights, and early mornings spent finishing the latest assignment, or studying for the next test, she began to feel excited. Excited because she was getting her degree and going to work.

In the end, it was with some degree of disappointment that she realized college would soon be over. In just two short years she had an associate's degree in social work. She was ready. Ready for a career.

Jax, in the meantime, had graduated from college with a Bachelor of Science in Finance, and took a job in Little Rock. To Gina, he looked just like his daddy, and was just as solid and dependable. Millie graduated the same spring, and she pleaded with both children to come home and spend the month of June with her.

This will probably be the last time we all have a chance to be together, just us three. I want one last time to enjoy both of my children at home.

They spent June together as a family, one last time – remembering Robert, making new memories, and enjoying the comfort of home. For all the changes in her life, for all the progress she had made, and for all the blessings she received, she gave thanks every day. She was so proud of her children and Robert would have been as well. Still, there was this small, empty place inside. Gina had much to be thankful for, and many friends and family that surrounded her, but something was missing.

As she looked back and remembered that month, and those memories, it seemed as if that life belonged to someone else. In a way it did. The woman that she was today barely resembled the woman of those years.

Gina went to work at the center in the fall of '99, as the Social Services Coordinator. For the next eleven years, she devoted herself to the undeserved and low-income residents of Polk County. It was Gina that helped to establish a range of social services, from mental health to drug rehabilitation. And it was the drug rehabilitation division that she finally called home her last six years at the Center. Methamphetamine was invading middle-class families, and from Gina's viewpoint, it was destroying a generation.

Nothing in her life, not even the loss of Robert, prepared her for the misery and devastation she witnessed as she struggled to help the people of her county. People who were having their lives ruined, either because they themselves were addicts or because one of their loved ones struggled with addiction. She couldn't remember how many times she had left work in tears. Tears shed for the families, for the addicts, or the sheer fact that their lives were such a mess.

Methamphetamine is a monster drug. Much akin to heroin,

breaking the physical and mental dependency is unbelievably hard. And the chemicals used to manufacture meth make physical changes to the brain itself; beyond that, it destroys the body. Nothing is left unaffected. She saw so many people that experienced real physical destruction because of the addiction. Heart attacks, strokes, loss of speech, neurological disorders--the list was endless. It became so hard to overcome her own feelings of despair as she dealt with person after person, and family after family.

Finally, when Gina was fifty-one, she went to the board and told them it was time for her to retire. Technology was changing, government oversight was changing, and all the while, Gina was losing her ability to cope with the emotions her work evoked. It was time to hand over the reins to someone younger, better qualified. She continued to work with some of her patients on a part-time volunteer basis, but that was as much as Gina was willing to do.

She had witnessed all the change she wanted. What she really wanted now was to go home and take some time for Gina. For so many years, she had been a wife, a mother, a friend, and a counselor. Now, she just wanted to be Gina.

Her first few months after retiring were a whirlwind. There were so many things she had put off until she had more time. Finally, when she had more time, she sometimes felt overwhelmed, and wondered how she ever managed to work and take care of a home. Somewhere along the way, she discovered social media. And with that discovery, a whole new world opened for her. One that allowed her to find friends, family, and old classmates.

That was how she stumbled upon Jo. Now, just a few short days after sending that friend request, they would have a chance to visit and try to find the remnants of a friendship. A friendship almost forty years neglected.

Yes, tomorrow will be another adventure for Jo and myself. It'll be an adventure for us just to find the girls we once were in the women we are today. That should take a little time, and a lot of conversation.

She turned out the light, and let the blissful emptiness of sleep take hold of her mind. Tomorrow was another day.

CHAPTER 8

The Straight and Narrow…is the hardest road to travel. Sometimes lonely, it is truly the road less travelled.

The straight and narrow, while requiring us to focus on our objectives and goals, also gives us the opportunity to achieve a dream.

Jo Felsenthal, Valedictorian Speech 1976

1976, Jo's Tomorrow's

THE LAST FEW WEEKS had been such a whirlwind. Robert and Gina, their marriage, graduating, receiving her letter from the Air Force, packing and preparing to leave, and then actually leaving. Her mind reeled from all the activity. Excitement pushed her forward. It was, after all, a great opportunity. One that she truly wanted to pursue – she hadn't thought about what the pursuit without Gina would look and feel like.

She spent her last Saturday at the co-op. She wanted to say good-bye to these wonderful people, people that she loved and cared for, people that were a part of her life in the Ozarks.

That Saturday, the co-op was filled with well-wishers, casual acquaintances, close friends, and finally, Mr. Clancy.

He waited until at last there was no one except him and Jo.

"Girl, you fixing to leave us, go out there and see what this ole world is all about. I got a a few partin' words for ya', just to make sure yer ready."

She smiled. She loved this old man. So solid, so much a part of the mountains, and so much a part of her co-op life.

"Yessir, I was hopin' you'd come to see me before I left. It wouldn't be right to leave without your advice. Whatcha got for me?"

"Well, I'm not gonna waste words: it's a man's world out there, Jo. An' you fixin' to step right off into the heart of it. The military has always been a man's world. These folks, they don't want no women; I done talked to Floyd and done some checkin' – they don't really want you there. An' when menfolk don't want no women in somethin', they can make it hard. Really unpleasant."

"Yessir, I know they don't want us there. I talked to my liaison officer about that, too."

"Well, he didn't tell ya what I'm gonna tell ya."

"Yessir. I know that, too." She smiled. He didn't mince words.

"One time, when I's a young man, I run up in a bad spot, no good way out. No sense in relatin' the details, just… there wadn't a good way outta what I was in. I knew I was fixin' to tote a whoopin', and it was gonna be a good 'en. I wasn't sure if I'd make it out. I was scared, so scared I pissed my pants, but I held my ground."

Jo listened intently.

"Anyway, you're fixin' to be in a bad spot. I don' think you're gonna haf' to worry about makin' it out, but it's gonna be unpleasant, real unpleasant at times. They gonna say things you never thought somebody sayin' to you-- things you ain't never heard a man say to a woman, or for that matter, do to a woman. I want ya' to know why. Why men will say things such as that. Strong women kinda scare men. You never know what they're gonna do, or say. You're the kinda woman that scares a man, Jo."

"You're strong, smart, free-spirited… wild, almost, like a bear, or a wolf in these here mountains. Untamed and unbroken. Whatever you do, girl, you don't forget what got you there. You're determined and smart as a whip. Stand your ground, don't let 'em break your spirit, and don't let 'em run you off."

"Mr. Clancy, they're not gonna run me off. I've worked too hard. I want this too much. I can do this. I know I can."

"I know you can too, but I also believe you're young and you don't truly understand what you're goin' to. Life don' give you but one chance. Don' wake up one mornin' regrettin' what might have been. See it through. Find out what's on the other side."

"An' don't never forget how much we love ya. We're always here, here with these mountains, here at home."

When he finished, he turned to go, tears welling in his eyes. They would miss each other. Jo found it hard to voice the goodbye that gegan forming on her lips. She reached to hug the old man, and he stopped long enough to return the embrace. Then he was gone. It was a conversation she would never forget, and would need in the weeks to come.

She left Little Rock at 10 a.m. June 26th. Time to report. Time to leave one life and start another. Robert and Gina were there to bid her goodbye, right along with the rest of her family. As she boarded the plane, she turned to smile one last time at Gina. *What am I gonna do without her?* She smiled and waved, hoping no one could see how scared she felt.

She was on her own for the first time in her life, and although she would never have admitted to anyone she loved, it was with more than a little trepidation that she stepped off the plane in Colorado Springs to begin her military life.

As she exited the plane, she reminded herself why she was here, why she had chosen the Air Force Academy. She wanted to experience the world, be free of the confining and small existence of Polk Ridge. She wanted to experience different countries, different continents, different people, and different cultures.

The young girl from the Ozarks was becoming a woman of the world. But as she stepped off the plane, and searched for her assigned contact, she once again felt overwhelmed. She had never flown in her life, and an airport is a busy place. She'd been instructed to search out Ms. Wiggins; she would be holding a sign with Jo's name on it. Ms. Wiggins would host her for the night, and promptly at 7, take her for "inprocessing" the next day.

As she entered the airport disembarking, sure enough, there was Ms. Wiggins, holding the sign. They exchanged hello's and introductions, and Ms. Wiggins took her to a phone so she could call her mom and dad, and then she was off – off to cadet life.

Ms. Wiggins was an Academy staff member, and as she explained to Jo on their way to her home, her life was going to change.

"You have no idea how hard this is going to be, Ms. Felsenthal. You young women are making history, and turning the military academies on their ear. The majority of the young cadets as well as the older officers were so against allowing females to come."

"Please call me Jo, Ms. Wiggins, and I already heard they didn't want the legislation to pass. Lt. Col Listermann, my liaison officer, told me about that."

"Well, I'm quite sure Lt. Col. Listermann didn't give you all the details. They don't have any accommodations for women. You're going to be staying in areas that were originally designed for men, and it will show. They didn't want to make it easy for women. And the language you're going to hear--it will be awful, Jo, really awful. They may have to abide by the law and let you in, but they don't have to be nice about it. If you fail, they're going to say 'I told you so.'"

"I'm not gonna fail." She stuck her chin out stubbornly, "I can do this, no matter what they say or do to me."

"I hope you're right, honey. I work in administration, so you'll find me around all the time, and if I can help you in any way, you let me know. This *is* going to be a tough first year for female cadets."

The next morning, as Ms. Wiggins drove her onto the organized chaos of the military installation, she wondered, once again, if she was ready to reach beyond the comfort of that small town. It all seemed loud, scary, and unwelcoming. She smiled to herself. She would adjust, adapt, and overcome. She was ready.

Inprocessing begins at Arnold Hall, a daylong event that each and every cadet completes. At Arnold Hall she received her clothing issue, room assignment, squadron assignment, an additional medical examination and review, and finally, it was time for the bus ride. Every cadet travels by bus to the "Bring Me Men Ramp." It is here that they truly begin cadet life. As she stepped off the bus, she scanned the footprints, imprinted in the concrete.

All cadets "step" into the footprints to signify that all are starting from the same place. She suddenly realized how deep tradition runs in the military. She also realized the first females were sweeping away an old tradition, and a new era was beginning.

The swearing-in ceremony was the moment she felt the true gravity and permanence of her choice. As she took the Oath of Allegiance, and swore to support and defend the Constitution of the United States, she became a cadet. A committed and devoted cadet, in every sense of the word.

She also became distinctly aware of one fact: Ms. Wiggins was right. Females were not a welcome addition to the Air Force Academy. Mr. Clancy's words of advice returned to play in her mind and over the next six weeks, and she began to understand what the old man had already known. She was in a tough spot.

Academy life is one of strict rules, hard work, dedication, commitment, and sometimes extreme physical exhaustion – especially for Jo in those first few weeks. Basic Cadet Training was a grueling process. Cadets must first complete BCT, which is the equivalent of a six-week vacation in hell. And basic training in the mountains around Colorado Springs was one of those memories she forever associated with the word "hellish;" it was in those grueling months of training that a woman was born from the young girl.

She often listened to her Superiors say it was "make or break" time, and as the summer came to a close, she fully understood exactly what that meant. There had been so many times it would have been much easier to simply give up, throw in the towel, and go home. Quitting wasn't what she came to do; she came to become an Air Force Officer, and if it took every ounce of her will, she was going to succeed.

During those weeks of training, she managed to make several friends among the other female cadets, and there was one in particular that she would remain in close contact with over the life of her career: Margaret Ann Wilson.

Margaret Ann, or "Maggie" as she preferred, was from Muscle Shoals, Alabama. She was as country as Jo. It was their "southern speech" and mountain roots, as well as the shared trials of female cadets that brought them together as friends and solidify a new friendship.

Muscle Shoals is located at the base of the Great Smokey Mountains, and borders the Tennessee state line. Maggie loved the mountains, the Air Force, and music. They shared so much in common.

During the music metamorphosis of the 1960's, a legendary

member of the music industry, Rick Hall, opened Fame Recording Studio. Famous bands and singers flocked to Muscle Shoals because of the unique acoustics, and as Maggie was quick to say, "the rest is history." She was particularly fond of an unknown band called Lynyrd Skynrd. She'd met them all, thanks to the fact that she had an uncle on her momma's side of the family, the Johnsons, who was involved with the recording studios.

Quite often, Jo would marvel at the "piece of work" that was Margaret Ann Wilson and turn to her for confidences and support when Academy life was overwhelming. She also found herself recalling much of Mr. Clancy's advice as she made her way through the Academy. He too, was a piece of work. She shared his words of wisdom with Maggie, much to Maggie's delight. She laughed often at the "sayings" that Jo seemed to effortlessly spout as they made their way through basic training.

She'd never before been tested to her physical and mental limits, but Basic Cadet Training and the hostility that she and her fellow female cadets faced during those first few weeks pushed her further than she ever thought she possessed the strength go.

The first three weeks of training, known as the "First Beast," consisted of instruction in military customs and heritage, knowledge skills testing, drills, and room inspections. At the end of the first phase, they competed against other squadrons in distance races, tug-of-war contests as teams, and log relays. Jo developed physically and mentally during this process, and managed to survive the transition from life as a civilian to that of a military cadet. It was her inner drive, her desire to succeed, and her commitment to her choice that helped her survive and persevere, even as they were warned to prepare for the "Second Beast" or the second three weeks of training in Jacks Valley.

Field Day exercises were finished, their squadron had performed extremely well, and Jo and Maggie had accumulated enough points to put them in the top twenty percent of the entire cadet class. Maybe this wasn't going to be as bad as she first thought.

"Maggie, all I want to do now is find a shower and a bed. I'm exhausted. I've got so much dirt, sweat, and mud on me that I feel like my grandpa's old sow."

"Yeah, me too. I want rest. Sweet, blissful, 'throw myself on the bed' rest."

"I know the next three weeks are gonna be worse than these first three, but I'm looking forward to being in the outdoors. Tent city can't be that bad."

"I don't know, Jo. I've listened to some of the guys talking, and it can get pretty rough out there. It's really physical, and I don't think the language is gonna improve that much either. I've been called everything from a good-for-nothing piece of trash to a whore, on and off the field, in and out of the classroom. I'm so sick of the mind games. The only reason I haven't taken it so hard is because they're doin' it to the guys too. My biggest issue is the fact that most of the guys don't want the women here, at all. I'm gonna stay and make it, mainly because they don't want us too."

"I know. I didn't realize people could be so prejudiced about a woman. I don't think my daddy did either. I know he wanted me to follow my dreams, but I don't think he realized how rough the language and actions of the Academy could get. Other than Mr. Floyd, Daddy's never been around that many military people."

"Aw, I know my momma and daddy didn't know any of this. Hell, the only thing Daddy's ever done is haul logs and work in the woods. You don't get many women out there, and the trees sure as hell don't cuss." She burst into laughter.

"No, my folks had no idea."

They reached their assigned quarters, and the heaven of a hot shower called to them. Tomorrow would be another day.

Jo only once questioned her decision to become an Air Force officer, and it was during the fifth week of the six weeks training. And that was at the Jacks Valley Encampment.

It was here they spent eighteen days living in a tent, while the upper-class cadets and commissioned officers tested them to the limits of their physical stamina and mental determination. If you could make it here, chances are you had the ability to survive the rest of the four years at the Academy.

Upon arriving, each new cadet had been instructed to erect their own individual tent. The acres of small tents became known as "tent city." Maggie and Jo were side by side, but separated by fifteen to twenty feet of open ground.

They had finished the third obstacle course and weapons skills training. The next day would bring their survival and endurance training in the mountains. Exhausted, the young women turned in as soon as they were turned loose. Out there, hygiene wasn't a primary concern, and most young cadets simply slept in the same clothes they would wear for the next day's exercises. Ready on a moment's notice.

Sometime during the early morning hours, Jo was awakened to the flap of her tent, moving as if someone were opening it. She sat up, aware that the mountains of Colorado could be dangerous, if for no other reason than the bobcats and bears. It was one of the upper-class cadets, Kirk Robertson.

"Cadet Felsenthal, c'mon, get up. We got an unexpected skills training event for you. C'mon, hurry." He spoke barely above a whisper.

Still half-asleep, she scrambled from her tent to find Kirk and two other upperclassman waiting for her a few feet from the tent. Motioning for her to be quiet, they waved for her to follow them. She did as she was directed, never realizing that "bad spot" Mr. Clancy had been talking about, waited just a few hundred yards from their "tent city."

Cadet Felsenthal never stood a chance. She never realized it was coming, not until it was too late. There were three of them, and only one of her.

As she slowly realized what was about to happen, her mind began to disconnect from the reality of the scene unfolding before her. Her home, her family, Gina, and Mr. Clancy beckoned her through the fog of disbelief, pain, and physical assault… *"We love you, girl, we're always here, come on home to the mountains..."*

Sometime after the assault, and somewhere through the fog that had enveloped her mind, she heard Kirk, as he leaned to whisper in her ear, "This is what Academy life is gonna be like for you split-tails!" Every word was laced with hatred and carefully constructed to instill fear and remind her that her place wasn't here.

Then she was alone.

After what seemed an eternity, but in reality was only an hour or so, she got up and walked back to her tent. Her mind reeling, her body bruised.

"This isn't happening. This isn't supposed to happen. This can't happen here. Not here." She quietly began to cry, and then as reality and fear released themselves, sobs racked her body. Almost magically, Maggie appeared at the opening to the tent.

"Felsenthal, what's wrong? I heard ya all the way…" She stopped mid-sentence to take a really close look at Jo.

"What happened to you? Ya' gotta be quiet. You're gonna wake up everybody else."

Through the tears, and the quiet stillness of the dawn, she shared the horror of the last few hours. Through those same tears and quiet stillness, Jo changed, and a different cadet greeted the sunrise.

Maggie left her only once, just long enough to retrieve the pack of Marlboro lights she had hidden in her bag. Compliments of Ms. Wiggins in Administration. She was a lady that understood their trials.

"If we're gonna be drug through hell, we might as well enjoy a smoke," and she tried at a half-hearted laugh.

"I know what you went through. It already happened to me." Jo's startled glance demanded an explanation. "No, not here. Before I got to the Academy, but the result is still the same. And the reason is pretty much the same. You do know why they're doin' this, don't you? It's because we're excelling. We're makin' it, we're doin' just as good as the guys. They don't want that, and they're gonna do everything they can to make it so bad, so hard we'll quit."

"What am I gonna do?"

"Well, you can report it. Buy why? What good's it gonna do? Unless you wanna quit. I ain't quittin' and I'm not gonna waste my time feelin' sorry for myself. It made me try harder. Nobody was gonna break me." With that, she gave Jo a long hard look. "And you don't let 'em get you either. We're survivors, and we will survive this, too."

"They gotta live with it, Jo. You'll be stronger, better and you'll have your day…ya knw what goes around comes around. They'll live to regret it. But it takes some time."

"Thanks, Maggie. Thank God you were here. I know now why Mr. Clancy was so worried. He probably already thought about what might happen. He just couldn't say it so plainly."

"Let me give you one more piece of advice. Take every ounce of that hurt, pain, and anger. Put it in an imaginary box and bury it. Bury it way down deep inside and someday, when you're far away from here, and in a safe place, take it out. Take it out, deal with it, and move on. But don't think about it anymore right now. Right now, let's just survive." Then she was gone.

Reporting an assault would have been the end of her opportunity at the Academy, and she knew it. She wasn't leaving, she wasn't giving up, and she would make sure that the "Kirks" of the Academy lived to regret their actions. Someway, somehow, someday. She simply needed to wait, wait for her chance.

Her parents came for the Acceptance Day Parade, and she had never been so glad to see them in her life. Finally, a living, breathing, reminder of the sweetness of home. She still had her dreams and her determination to see the world, but she also had a much better appreciation for the life she'd left at home.

"Mom, Dad, oh my gosh! I'm so glad to see you two!" she called as she raced to embrace them. It was a heartfelt embrace, tinged with just a little desperation.

They both noticed the change to "Mom" and "Dad," not "Momma" and "Daddy." Much had changed about Jo in the last six weeks. She didn't really feel like their little girl anymore. She felt like their daughter, their battle-hardened, severely tested, and changed adult daughter.

"Hey, sweetheart. My how nice, all dressed up in those military blues. We're so proud of you." It was Maureen that spoke. Tom was studying his daughter's face. Looking for signs of distress, or worse – abuse.

"I want you to meet Maggie. She's from Muscle Shoals. Her parents couldn't come. It was too far, so if you don't mind, I invited her to spend her family time with us."

Maggie walked over to them. She was taller than Jo, with brown hair and eyes. Slender and graceful with her steps, she extended a warm hand to Jo's parents. She met Tom's gaze with the same look

Jo had worn. He kept his thoughts to himself, but Maggie knew what he was thinking. She'd seen that expression before.

We're already fighting a battle. A battle just to be accepted. At least we've got each other.

"You had to cut that beautiful auburn hair, I see. But otherwise, you still look like my baby girl. I don't suppose yours was this short either Maggie when you got here?"

"No, sir, they shaved us up pretty good."

They enjoyed a laugh, and both young women relayed stories of their cadet training: the rigors of the mountains, and the strict, regimented routine of cadet life.

Towards the end of their visit, her dad pulled her to the side.

"Jo, you look beautiful in those military clothes, but you look a little tired, or sad. Are you making it okay? Are they treating you girls good? It's not too late to change your mind and come home. You know we love you, whether you're an Air Force officer or just our daughter. Are you sure you wanna stay?"

Her daddy knew her too well. He'd picked up on what she had tried so hard to hide behind her smile and conversation.

"Yes, daddy. I'm stayin'. I've gone through too much already to give it up. They may not cotton to us bein' here, and they may make it hard, but they're not gonna kill us. I don't think they've got the 'balls' to kill us!" She laughed as she saw the shock on his face, and then he managed to join her in the laughter. Yes, his little girl was definitely changing!

When it was time to go, they were reluctant to part, but duty called, and the girls said their goodbyes.

"Dad," Jo began, "I love y'all, and for what it's worth, you and Mom have been great parents. There's so much that I learned growing up, and it's been a comfort these last few weeks. I just wanted you to know. And will you tell Gina and Mr. Clancy I said hi?"

When she began the process for applying to the Academy, the questionnaire she completed asked so many questions. Most of them were pertained to her life up until her senior year. Some of them, however, focused on her goals and ambitions: What did she want to study? Where did she want to go? What motivated her to join the military?

She finally had the opportunity to give real thought to a career. Something that had never been the focus of her attention. What *did* she want to study? She knew little about her career options, but she did love math and science. In fact, Jo was passionate when it came to math. She loved the clarity of numbers. With a math equation, the answer was always a clear choice, no fuzzy "what if's"; two plus two was always four. It was finally her conversation with her math teacher that had helped her make a career choice. It would be engineering.

And although she had no way of knowing, it was this excellence and passion in mathematics that was going to land her a tremendous opportunity. One that opened doors and thrust her into a career that was on the leading edge of technology. The Internet was coming. Much of the work and research that would, in just a few short years, be the greatest commercial innovation since the industrial revolution, was being conducted in the military as a way to communicate globally between military powers.

The "internetworking" was under development and several European countries, as well as the U.S. military, were participating. The term "internetworking" later became shortened to "internet," and the information-sharing revolution would be born, right along with a career for Jo.

As she prepared to enter her fourth class cadet year at the Academy, she was given several aptitude tests by the Air Force. Their primary purpose: discover her true strengths and weaknesses so that her time at the Academy would be most beneficial for her, as well as the military. When she received her academic assessment results and was called in to the dean's office, she was unprepared for the team of faculty, advisors, and officers that awaited her.

Once in the room and seated, the Dean explained to Jo that in addition to her expected curriculum for fourth class cadets, she had been chosen to participate on a "new and highly technical" team developing a system of global communication. It was a joint effort involving all branches of the U.S. military, as well as Germany, France, Sweden, and Norway.

She was assigned to work with two other fourth-class cadets, two upper-class cadets, a handful of military faculty, and a liaison from ARPANET. They were developing a system of networks for computing, relaying and switching information transfers between geographically distant locations. Although she had never heard of a computer, the systems under development that were called "computing" information systems, would soon become known as computers, and terms such as TCP/IP, megabytes, and routers were being born.

She also had no way of knowing the importance the computer would play in years to come, but she did realize the opportunity she was being given. She felt a rush of excitement as each person in the room explained his or her role in the team's work. The Dean finally spoke again with a last piece of information. Information that exploded like a bomb in Jo's head.

"Cadet Felsenthal, as you are aware, we have never accepted female cadets in the long and storied history of the U.S. Military. There has never been a need nor did we foresee the need to enroll women as officers. However, it is now a legal requirement for all branches, and we, just as the others, are accommodating those requirements.

Having said that, I want you to know that you wouldn't be on this team if you weren't deserving. You have managed to prove to everyone involved in your training, that you are a very capable cadet, one of the best and brightest.

"Your math scores on the aptitude test were astonishing, considering the limited classroom instruction you've received. It was for this reason, and the fact that you excelled during your BCT, that we chose you for this opportunity."

"You will be a part of a five-man team. Your fellow cadet, Margaret Ann Wilson, and upperclass cadets Kirk Robertson, John Haskins, and Will Johnson. I expect nothing less than excellence and achievement from this team. In fact, Cadet Robertson commended you and Cadet Wilson. He said you went above and beyond during the field exercises."

"Yessir, I won't let you down."

Her mind reeled from the information she'd been given. The last of which she couldn't believe.

I bet he did. I bet that wasn't all he said either. I even bet he had something to do with my position on the team. Well, screw him. I am one of the best and brightest. This is his undoing, not mine. But dammit, I have to work on a team with this asshole.

The last several weeks of training had sharpened her mentally, emotionally, and physically. She knew she was ready for her responsibilities as a member of the team. She could and would excel as a member of the team. It was working with Kirk that might be the problem. Well, like it or not, if she wanted to stay, she would have to find a way to deal with his presence.

If there was anything she knew how to do, it was to compete in the classroom. She would have her chance to even the score with Kirk Robertson; she was willing to bet her future on it.

It didn't take long for the opportunity to present itself. Kirk might be a man with the upper hand because of gender, but he was no match for her in mathematics and computations. She excelled when it came time to determine what kind of calculations could be performed, and the speed with which they could be completed with the systems they were developing. On more than one occasion, she outperformed her male counterparts, Kirk included. Soon, it was Jo they begrudgingly gave credit for much of the progress in calculating processing times. She began to feel that she was earning the respect of her cadet peers, if not necessarily settling a score. She was the best and the brightest, and it was evident in the classroom, and in her teamwork.

The next four years of her life flew by, and her participation on the development and implementation of internet protocols, interface message processors, switching software, and networks put her in a rare position: a position that could take her all over the world, afford her the opportunity to work with people from tremendously varied backgrounds, and fulfill a young girl's dream of different countries, different continents, and different languages.

When she graduated from the Air Force Academy, she had majored in computer and network security, and had minors in the languages of German, French, and Norwegian. To say that she excelled in academics would have been an understatement, and to say that she had anything left in common with Gina would have been a complete myth.

She hadn't returned home very often over the course of her years at the Academy, and of the two visits she had made, she hadn't stopped by to see Gina. They exchanged letters quite frequently during her first couple of years at the Academy, but as she became more involved in her military education and career, she had less and less to share with Gina, and Gina had less to share with her. Finally, when she graduated, it had been almost two years since they had written.

After graduation, each cadet received sixty days of paid leave, and then it was off to their first commission. Jo's first commission, or "assignment" as her mom liked to say, would be in Germany. Tom and Maureen wanted to have the family together to visit with her on her last trip home before leaving. It gave them the opportunity to be proud parents, share their youngest daughter's achievements, and she'd get to see everyone and visit, all at once, all in one place. To their disappointment, she spent only two weeks of her leave at home in Polk Ridge. The urge to see things in the world was still pulling on Jo.

From there, she was going to Muscle Shoals to spend a week with Maggie. She wanted to see the Smokey Mountains that Maggie had talked about so much during their time at the Academy, and she wanted to see Fame Studios. She had become quite a fan of Lynyrd Skynrd.

Then, it was on to Germany. She planned to get there two weeks ahead of the date she was to report, in time to explore the many tourist attractions she had only ever heard recounted through Gina. There was so much she wanted to see and do now that she had her education, a career and a chance to realize her dreams.

Stella, her husband Jack, Gina, and Robert and their two children, and Floyd and Louise, were invited the Saturday night before she left on Sunday. Even Mr. Clancy was invited.

Her visit, however, wasn't going to give her the opportunity to see her friend. Thanks to a sick baby, and an even sicker Gina, one more chance to cross paths slipped away.

Germany turned out to be everything Jo had envisioned and then some. She loved her work, she loved the country, but mostly, she loved her freedom. There was so much to see, so much to do. As she worked and visited in Germany, she thought about Gina. She knew that this was where she had been born, and quite often wondered if she had walked some of the same halls, or visited some of the same buildings. Thanks to the many conversations they had shared, she was all too familiar with the historical and tourists spots Gina had visited, and while she was there, made it a point to see them firsthand.

She was involved in some of the most exciting work ever experienced in the military. It was the greatest development in communication since the invention of telephones, and 2nd Lt. Felsenthal led a special team in Germany charged with establishing network connectivity on the U.S. Air force base in Spangdahlem.

The first three years flew by. The team had accomplished much of their assigned tasks as they approached the final year. The last of their work that remained required interface with German infrastructure, and that was proving to be a nightmare. Quite often, Jo and several of the other officers found themselves sharing a drink at the Officer's Club, commiserating about the "joy" of dealing with a foreign country and the issues they had to overcome.

The Officer's Club was a safe haven for personnel on base, one because it provided them with a place to socialize with peers, and two because it could have been located on any base, anywhere. It was a familiarity in lives that were often filled with unfamiliar places and people. The Officer's Club in Spangdahlem was a rather small, dimly lit place decorated to emphasize the German culture with pictures of previous accomplished Air Force officers hung sporadically on the walls. Here, they would meet and share the days' events, good or bad.

It was on just such an occasion late one Tuesday afternoon that fate decided it was time to even a score.

Jo and some of the 2nd Lt's on her team sat at a table, discussing their latest "challenges" when Jo noticed the door open and then close behind a male figure. Since the comings and goings of people from the Officer's Club was much like that of any other bar, they paid very little attention to the traffic. The lights were dim, and they weren't that interested.

She continued her conversation, right up until she heard a familiar voice behind her, "Hello, 1st Lt. Felsenthal. Mind if I join you?"

Jo's entire body seemed to stop – her thoughts, even the air in her lungs seemed to collapse for a few brief seconds.

"No, sir, you're more than welcome to join us," she finally responded.

As he sat down to join them, he turned to the bartender. "Can I get another round for the table?"

Jo began to protest; she had no intention of staying to share drinks with the Major Kirk Robertson.

The other officers at the table, either because they were uncomfortable with the Major, or because they sensed that there was more here than a friendly drink, quickly excused themselves. Between the arrival of the drinks, and the excuses of the other officers, she didn't manage to escape.

"Well, she drawled, in her most slow southern cadence, "you've got some kinda nuts. Only someone as yellow as you could manage to slither into the Officer's club to harass a female officer. She emphasized the word "female." Then she smiled, the most beautiful and deadly smile she could muster, but her words were laced with sarcasm. "I am not going to sit here with you. You can have the damn drink." She rose to leave.

"Jo, wait just one minute. Please. I need to say something, something I've needed to say for a couple of years now. Just give me five minutes of your time, and then if you want, you never have to talk to me again."

She stopped to look down at him. Why should she give him anything but a bullet between the eyes?

"Alright. I'll give you five minutes, but no more. And you don't deserve that." Her voice was flat, devoid of emotion.

He nodded and started to talk.

"Three years ago, I got married. I married a woman I met while I was in Altus, Oklahoma. A sweet, kind, and caring woman." He paused. "She has auburn hair, too."

So why do I care? I hope she cuts the son-a-bitch off. I don't give a damn about her hair. He continued to talk, oblivious to her thoughts or the blank stare she gave him.

"Two years ago we were in Washington, D.C. I needed to attend a meeting one night, and I left her alone. Alone in a strange place. She didn't know anyone there, and decided to go across the street from the hotel for a quick supper. On her way back, she was attacked and raped."

The words landed as pieces of lead on Jo's ears. The old fear, the old anger began to rise, trying to bubble to the top. *He's suffering, just like I did, just like she did. Maggie… she was right.*

"I couldn't save her. I couldn't even help her like I should have, because the only think I could think about was the fact that I had been the same kind of animal. I was no better than the man that attacked my wife. And for the first time, I saw from the other side what I did to you. I saw through the eyes of the woman I loved the devastation and destruction I inflicted on you." He stopped at that point to take a drink. His eyes hollow and haunted.

"We divorced last year. And in so many ways, I blame myself. I just couldn't get past my own issues to help her deal with hers. Since then, I've known I needed to find you, to say how sorry I am for what I did to you. No apology can fix what I did. No effort on my part can undo what I did. But I needed you to know that if I could, I would. I would recall anything and everything I did to you that night. I hope someday, somehow, you can forgive me for what I did, but if you can't, I understand that too."

Jo sat transfixed. Maggie's words played through her mind: *"Ya know, what goes around comes around."* She also realized something else: all the pain, all the hurt, even a lot of the anger, was gone. She felt just as hollow about that night, as his eyes looked sitting across the table.

"Kirk…" She didn't even bother with "Major." "I'm sorry for your wife, I'm sorry for you, and for a long time, I was sorry for me. But I need to tell *you* something as well. The next couple of days after that happened, I felt violated, cheated, destroyed and I really felt like I was your 'victim;' then I realized that as long as I felt that way, I gave you power over my life."

"You didn't deserve that. You certainly didn't earn it, and I refused to give it to you. Now today, I'm sitting across the table from the real victim. *You* are the victim of your own actions, and you'll have to live with that for the rest of your life."

With those final words, she stood and left the Major. She left him, sitting alone with his thoughts and his remorse. He would have to live with the consequences of his choices. One simple choice that altered the course of their lives. She was stronger. He was weaker.

As soon as she made it back to her apartment, she dialed Maggie. She had to let her know what had happened. She was right; justice will eventually be served. She was truly sorry for his wife. She was just an innocent woman, a woman that had been assaulted and violated, something Jo understood all too well. But Kirk, he deserved whatever he got.

"Maggie, you got a minute? You remember Jacks Valley and your advice about what goes around comes around? Well, tonight it came around…"

From Germany, she went to France. This time, Maggie went with her.

It was just what Jo needed: the company of a friend. The two women made it a point to enjoy as much of the French culture as time allowed. The food, the wine, and the romantic atmosphere. Paris was their favorite spot; more specifically, the Eiffel Tower and the Altitude.

Jo remembered the pictures from one of Gina's scrapbooks, and every time she and Maggie visited, she thought of her. They were working on ten years apart, and Jo wondered what her life was like now. She and Robert would be married ten years and raising two children.

I can't imagine how that would be. A husband and kids. I'm nowhere near ready for that. Not right now. My life is too full with work and travel.

From France it was on to Japan. As she travelled, she wrote her dad. She had very few friends to share her deepest thoughts, hopes, and dreams with, so she turned to the man that had not only been her parent and advisor, but her friend as well. During those first few years, it was more for advice, but as the years passed, it became her release, and a way to share. She and her dad were cut from the same cloth. He understood so much about his daughter's free spirit, her strength of will, and her passionate desire to see the world.

Although his world never exceeded the boundaries of Polk Ridge, he was more than willing to listen to Jo's stories. As she travelled and lived in places he could only dream of, he lived through her stories. She was his eyes and ears. For all the years that she'd been gone, she had written letters to her Dad, long letters that detailed as much as she could about her work and her travels.

As time passed, and she had less time to write, they shared phone conversations that served as the link between them. He was the lifeline she needed to remind her that there were people who loved and missed her, and were interested in her life.

An officer's life for a young woman was turning out to be demanding and full. Jo's lifestyle left her little time for a husband or family of her own.

Why did I let so many chances pass me by? Was it because of Jack Valley, or was it because of Paul?

Some part of her hadn't reconciled her place in Paul's life, then or now. She didn't even know where he was or what he was doing. But she could at last be honest with herself. She had loved Paul then, and somewhere deep down inside, she still did.

She sighed. *That chance was lost so long ago.* His words that night at the iron bridge, replayed in her head.

"I can wait, Jo. I can wait 'til you see what you gotta see, if you can just tell me you'll come back, I can wait."

But she didn't come back. She couldn't. She wasn't finished with all that she wanted to do, see, and experience.

CHAPTER 9

CAPT. JORJA FELSENTHAL ARRIVED in Japan in the spring of 1991, and was once again in charge of a team of computing specialists. This time, however, their mission was not simply military in nature. Coordination and work with Japanese businesses was involved.

She had been chosen for two reasons: one, because she was one of the military's best and brightest in her field and had already been in charge of three installations, and two, she had studied the Japanese language, their culture and customs extensively. She was the most well-positioned militarily and personally to work as a liaison with the Japanese industries to promote the goal of computer connectivity in a controlled experiment that was designed to test the commercial use of the internet.

She was, at this point, a woman with a career, and reaping the benefits of a successful military life. At thirty-three, she truly was at the top of her field.

A normal day for Jo began at 4:30 a.m. Up with a cup of coffee and a cigarette, she managed to dress and be out the door of her military base housing by 5:30, ready to report for work by 6. By July, she had things well in hand, and she could see she was making great strides with the implementation.

On this particular Friday, July 7th, she had scheduled meetings with military personnel and Japanese businessmen until noon. As usual, she instructed her assistant to hold any and every call, with no interruptions, until the meetings were complete. That morning, however, life would prove that some things just cannot go as planned, even if you are Jo Felsenthal and have a meticulously scheduled agenda.

Many miles and several continents away, Tom Felsenthal began his previous day as usual. Up and off to the co-op by 6, the day was in full swing – it was summer in the Ozarks, and time for crops to come in. This meant he would be busy on the yard, and any office work simply had to wait until that night. By 8 a.m., he knew something wasn't right; he was having trouble with his vision, and several farmers had already asked if he was alright, they were having trouble understanding his sentences.

Shortly before 10 a.m., he called Maureen to come to the co-op. He needed her to drive him home. By the time she arrived, she knew home wasn't an option and took him straight to Flowood. The emergency medical facility was thirty-five minutes away; it was almost too far for Tom.

As soon as she could, Maureen placed a call to Gina. She'd been trying to get Stella, but couldn't. She asked her to keep trying. She had to return to the ICU. Finally, Gina had gotten her on the phone.

Stella called her mom mid-afternoon, and told her as soon as she could get ahold of Jo that she would be on her way. It took Stella a few minutes to remember where she had put the number. Finally, she dumped the junk drawer out on the floor and found it.

She placed the international call to Jo and waited to be connected.

As soon as Jo's assistant answered the phone, Stella launched into the details of her situation, and told her she desperately needed to speak to her sister.

Meeting or not, the call went through, and her meticulously planned morning was turned upside down with a few short words from Stella.

"Jo, something's wrong with Daddy. He's at the hospital. Momma had to go get him at the co-op this morning. I just talked to her, and she said they don't know what it is yet, but it's not good. He can't talk, and by the time she got 'em to the hospital, he could barely walk."

"Oh, no, not Daddy, not now, I'm so far away... what do I need to do?"

"Jo, I think the only thing you can do right now is come home as fast as you can."

"Oh, Stella, I can't believe this. Not Dad. He's never been sick, never. I'll get a flight, and I'll be there as soon as I can. It's gonna take at least twenty-four hours. Tell Momma I'm coming, but it's gonna take some time. I'll call as soon as I can get to a phone. And..." Her voice broke. "Tell daddy I'm coming." She never thought to ask what hospital, but she figured she knew. Flowood. It would have been the closest.

It took her only twenty-two hours, thanks to a military flight and her captain's rank to get home. Once she got to Little Rock, however, it was another hour to her dad. She stopped only long enough to call her Mom at the hospital. It was a shaky Maureen that answered the phone in the ICU waiting room.

"Momma, it's me, Jo. I'm in Little Rock. How is he?"

"Oh, Jo. It ain't good, honey. You need to hurry."

She almost didn't make it. He had suffered a massive stroke--an AVM, according to the doctor. He was lucky to have lived at all. He made it just long enough for her to say goodbye.

Fatigue, the emotional rollercoaster, and sheer devastation overtook Jo; she had never prepared herself to experience one of her parents' death, and all the training and education in the world can't help you at a time like that. She felt lost and alone. She loved her Mom, but her Dad had been her lifeline, her friend. It was in him that she confided her accomplishments, hopes, and dreams. Now he was gone.

Just like Gina. She thought of her old friend, but too much time had passed; there would be no real comfort that she could give her now.

When she got home, home to the mountains, she quietly slipped from the house. It took her only a few minutes to find that magical spot, and then she let the tears flow. Tears for her dad, tears for a life that had taken her away for so many years, and tears that would hopefully wash away some of the hurt, pain, and loss.

Those days were a blur for her: the funeral and the family that she saw were more like pieces of a half-remembered dream, a mirage. First there was the viewing, so many people, so much sorrow. She only vaguely remembered seeing Gina, it was such an overwhelming time. The doctor had given her mother and Stella a sedative. But Jo had refused. She didn't want to ease the impact of the loss. She needed to remember her final days with her dad, even if it was only his body that was there.

Then came the funeral the next day. They laid him to rest in pouring rain, and thunderstorms.

The weather feels like I do on the inside: stormy and raining sadness.

Only after returning to Japan, and her daily routine, was she be able to put the event in perspective and try to overcome the feelings of grief and loss.

She lost more than a father; she lost a friend. For only the second time since high school she felt truly lonely, and questioned the lack of a real personal relationship in her life beyond that of her family. It was at this low point that she met Brigadier General Phillip Smart. Maybe it was the loss, or maybe it was just that her heart was ready; it was a question she never bothered to answer.

She heard her dad often during those days: "It's always darkest before the dawn, Jo." The loss of her dad was her darkness, but what would bring the dawn? He was never going to return. How could there be a brighter day, if he was never returning?

Time. Time brought her a brighter day. Time, and the arrival of someone else to fill her need for friendship and respect. Someone to share her thoughts with about her work, and to feel a stirring of emotion. That someone would be Phillip Smart.

Brigadier General Phillip Smart reached Japan almost a year after her assignment began. They met at a formal dinner that was meant to welcome the new Brigadier General and introduce him to many of the military and civilian personnel he would be working with while assigned to Kadena Air Force Base in Okinawa.

For much of that evening, however, Phillip spent his time getting to know Jo, and even though seating was prearranged for events such as this, Phillip managed to move her so that she spent much of the evening either in conversation with him, or dining beside him.

For a woman, she was rather tall at 5' 5", but Phillip Smart was a good six inches taller than her, with blond hair and dark brown eyes. She hadn't felt such overpowering emotion since Paul Collections. It was his eyes that first ignited her interest. Then the conversation managed to hold her interest. After the meal, he excused himself, and Jo knew as he walked away that she was in trouble.

As she was about to leave, he hailed her once again.

"Jo, where can I find you tomorrow?"

"Before I get off work, or after?" she asked. He looked at her with those piercing dark eyes. "After."

Those eyes… they seemed to see into her very soul, and she was never too sure of herself in his presence. Even after a year of dating, Jo sometimes caught him watching her. Never too sure what thoughts lay behind those deep brown eyes.

For every ounce of intelligence that she possessed in the communications and network security arena, Phillip Smart was her equal in navigation and combat air tactics. He was a military pilot, with twenty years invested in the Air Force, in tactical air control.

Well-respected and extremely intelligent, Jo found herself completely enamored with Phillip and well on her way to falling in love. He was ten years her senior, but that never seemed to matter to either of them.

He was quite athletic, and although Jo hadn't started life as an athlete, her years of military training had managed to keep her physically fit, and quite capable when it came to outdoor recreation. They ran, swam, and enjoyed tennis and beach volleyball in their off time. It was the conversation, however, that excited her most. They talked for hours, not only as friends, but as military officers. Their combined knowledge kept their conversations lively and entertaining. It seemed to Jo that she had finally found a partner.

Partnering, however, when you are military officers, is quite a complicated issue.

Phillip was sent to Kadena for a two-year assignment; Jo, who had already been there a year when he arrived, was at the Kadena base for a scheduled four-year assignment. That meant that he would be reassigned before her time was complete. As the first year turned into the second year, they began to discuss what a yearlong separation would mean, and how they could handle a long-distance relationship. Neither of them were too sure how well it would, or if it could work.

"You know, it's gonna be hard to live on a different continent and try to have a relationship. Can you wait for me, Phillip?"

She was never quite satisfied with the answer she got. She never felt good about the "sure, Jo" she got when she asked the question. At least she had been honest with Paul. If Phillip couldn't wait, she wanted to at least hear the truth.

It was the fall of 1993, and the conflict in Bosnia was still a problem for the United Nations and NATO forces. Phillip was being reassigned early, to Italy. His expertise in air combat tactics was desperately needed to try to bring a situation still teetering on "out of control" under some semblance of control. There needed to be some progress between Bosnia and Herzegovina.

The hurried transfer left them little time to prepare. It was an unexpected separation, and she would look back with regret that she had never uttered those three words when they parted. "I love you" would have been so easy to say, and yet she had refrained. Afraid that he didn't feel the same, or that he wasn't yet ready to share those feelings with her. She remembered those last few days, and learned a valuable lesson when it came to seizing the moment; once it passes, it may never come again. For Jo and Phillip, it would not come again.

He would never return to her from that assignment, and her heart never seemed to fully recover. As the years passed, and the assignments came and went, and she moved from country to country, and airbase to airbase, she found other lovers, but never another love. She had fallen in love twice: first with Paul, then with Phillip. For Paul she couldn't wait; with Phillip, he wouldn't wait. Life was such an ironic place.

Just as she was trying to recover from Phillip, Maggie managed to make her way back. This time, however, she had a husband in tow.

"Capt. Wilson, it's about time you decided to show up for some real work. I thought you were still in Alabama at Maxwell. When did you get here?"

Maggie had popped into Jo's office, completely out of the blue that afternoon, grinning widely and looking as if she were the cat that ate the canary.

"Well, I was until last month, then I was 'asked' to come over here for a couple of years." She laughed. "Does the Air Force ever really *ask*?"

It was at that moment that Jo noticed the ring on her left hand.

"Maggie, you got married! Why in hell didn't you tell me? When did this happen? Who is it? Is he military?"

"Slow down, Jo." And the giggling began. "I can't answer everything all at once. It happened two months ago. I didn't tell you because it was rather sudden and I didn't have much time to tell anybody. His name is James Johnson. Jimmy is what everybody calls him. And no, he's not military. He's from Muscle Shoals, too. Did that get 'em all?"

She was grinning from ear to ear.

"Johnson. Wasn't your momma's folks Johnsons?"

"Well, yes, and we're a little kin, but he's so good-looking, you just gotta meet him. He's coming in a couple of weeks, so you two can visit then. I'm happy, and we're such a good fit. He just loves that we'll get to travel, and…"

Jo interrupted. "Are you sure this is what you wanna do? I mean, it's a little late now, but are you sure being married is what you want?"

At that, Maggie stopped and looked at Jo solemnly. Her smile vanished.

"Yes," she said softly. "I'm sure, Jo. I'm sure I'm tired of being alone. Tired of not having somebody like Jimmy. He loves me, he's good to me, and I'm tired of going home to an empty house."

Jo understood all too well what Maggie was telling her. She never questioned her friend again about her reasons for marrying. She knew about going home to an empty house.

Somehow, even with all the moves between bases and continents, Jo managed to make several close friends. Maggie was one, and George Durand was another. George had been with her during Germany, and then again when she was commissioned at Edwards Air Force Base in California. It was in California that they became such close friends.

He was from Convent, Louisiana, a fact that you could discern the first time you engaged him in conversation, and it was also one of the reasons Jo liked him. He was from home and she didn't encounter many officers with southern roots. She also learned to respect him, he truly deserved the title of the "best and brightest;" he knew more about cyber-security than anyone she had ever encountered. And thanks to that friendship, she found her next opportunity in life.

Major Jo Felsenthal had devoted herself to the military for almost twenty-five years when she finally decided it was time to retire. She was ready to hang up her military blues for some civilian jeans, and spend a little more time stateside. She wasn't really ready to completely stop working, not yet. But she was almost fifty years old, and it was time to slow down. She could have retired at twenty years, but thanks to her knowledge of network and cyber-security, she had been asked to stay an additional five. Now that those years were complete, she put in her papers. Time to give it up.

As soon as she put in for her retirement, she placed a call to George. He had himself retired some three years earlier, and every time they talked, he offered Jo a job as a cyber-specialist with an independent contractor. She asked if he was ready to make good on the offer.

"Hi, George. How's everything in D.C.?

"Jo! Hellish, my dear friend. Hellish. How's everything… er, where are you now?'

She laughed. He never even tried to keep up with her whereabouts.

"It doesn't matter. I just put in my papers. I'm headed back to the USA. That offer you made a few months ago still good?"

"Jesus, yes! When can you be here? Tomorrow? That might not be soon enough. Those damn Chinese are gonna be the death of us, and it gets worse every day."

"George, you know I can't be there tomorrow, but how about the first of next month? It'll take sixty days for processing, but I need to come to D.C. and check things out, before it's time to actually pack up and move. August 3rd sound good to you? And by the way, where do I need to meet you?"

"You can meet me at the Pentagon. I'll email you the exact location, as well as the information on the contractor you'll be working for. Mom and Dad will be here that week as well, so I may be kind of busy after work. These two should never be alone in the nation's capital. I'm never too sure what they're gonna do, or what kind of mess I'll need to clean up."

"Oh, c'mon. George. They can't be that bad – how old are they?"

"They're in their seventies, but it's not their age that's the problem. It's their dissatisfaction with their government, and their hippie roots. When you combine the two, you've got all the makings for 'disturbing the peace' or 'disorderly conduct' charges. They only come every three or four years, mostly because Dad says D.C. is a 'den of iniquity, liars and thieves' – a point I can't argue – and he wants to make sure that I'm not converting to the other side. Once we visit for a couple of days, we're both ready to say our goodbyes. You know, I went to see them once, some godforsaken place in Missouri. Come to think of it, it might be pretty close to Polk Ridge. Anyway, I never wanted to go back – no Internet, no bars, and no air conditioning – no need to return." Jo laughed. She would enjoy seeing George again.

The rest of the conversation covered everything from hacking issues to the weather in D.C., and she wasn't ready to hang up when he had to go. She heard the persistent ring of the office phone in the background.

"Oh, hell. Gotta go, Jo--duty calls. See ya in a few weeks!" Then he was gone.

She hadn't been too sure about his offer at first, but the more she researched and thought about the opportunity, the more she wanted to make a change. D.C. might be exactly what she needed.

He had explained several times over in previous conversations that network and cyber security were top priorities at the Department of Defense, and they could definitely use someone with her skill set. So it was, in August of 2000, that she found herself in the nation's capital, in ninety-degree weather and wilting humidity to meet with George and the contractor.

The Pentagon is an imposing building, no matter where you enter and exit. Jo had visited on more than one occasion, but each and every time, it managed to take her breath. It was truly astounding at the superior air this place gave to visitors as well as military personnel. It seemed to say, "Yes, I house the greatest military in the world. Come and be impressed."

Officially, the Pentagon is in Arlington, Virginia. In reality, it overlooks Washington, D.C. from across the Potomac River. It's hard to distinguish where one stops and the other begins.

As she entered the building, she pondered her situation, and her years of travel. She'd been given great opportunities, and she had travelled the world just as she had wanted, but was she happy? Was this what she really wanted? Had things turned out for her has she had envisioned? In so many ways, the answer was yes, and yet she felt such a gnawing feeling, an emptiness inside.

Funny how I've managed to let so much of my roots slip away, slip away as I traded family and closeness for the promise of travel and adventure and work. I've dedicated my life to my work and never noticed that so many of the ones I love have slipped out of my grasp… gone like the leaves of November. And what do I have now? Maybe it's time to go home… to the mountains, to Polk Ridge.

What's wrong with you? Stop feeling sorry for yourself. You have a great life, you're one of the best in your field, you have opportunity; you should be on top of the world. Stop this nonsense. Move on. Polk Ridge isn't going anywhere.

The elevator gave the slight "ding" to indicate she'd arrived at her chosen floor, and as the doors opened, she pushed the pity thoughts to the back of her mind. Time to see George!

Jo spent the next ten years or so working for a private contractor, work she managed to enjoy. She was an expert in her field, and it was evident in her work. Work and her life were stimulating, busy places. Working alongside George once again, they made tremendous progress in writing code and creating software systems aimed at thwarting cyber "warfare" attacks. They weren't alone – there was a virtual army of contractors and employees working on issues that threatened the very security of the military and the nation.

She shuddered when she thought about that terrible day in September 2001. That single event had turned their work into more of a covert mission than a regular job. Progress had been made, but it wasn't near enough.

Jo normally took lunch at the Center Courtyard Café, taking care to return each day with something for George. His eating habits were atrocious! One day, during her fifth year in D.C., she took the elevator down to go to lunch. As it reached the bottom floor, and the doors slid apart, they opened to the face of Margaret Ann.

"Oh my God, what are you doin' here?" Jo exclaimed. Maggie had retired after putting in her twenty and moved back to Muscle Shoals. Although they talked often on the phone, she didn't know that Maggie was in Washington, or even planning a visit.

"Well, that husband of mine decided to up and die two weeks ago, and I just couldn't take it anymore. All that crying and carrying on… his momma is a complete wreck, my momma's a complete wreck; I had to leave. I needed to get out for a while, and you were the first thing that came to mind, so here I am."

Jo stopped in midstride.

"Good God, Maggie! *Jimmy* died? Was he sick? Why didn't you call me? I would've come for the funeral. I could've done *something* for you. You should've called."

"You're from a small town. You know how it is when somebody dies. Everybody wants to know everything, everybody comes to see you, everybody brings food... hell, I didn't have time to call you. I was too busy answering the door."

Jo laughed. She was never one for mincing words.

"Well, c'mon. I was on my way to lunch. Let's go eat, tand hen we can make some plans. How long are you stayin'? Where are you stayin'? How did you know where to find my office?"

Jo, it's 2005. Tou ever hear of the Internet?" At that she cackled loudly.

Apparently, Maggie did have time to call George before she left for Washington, and she had no intention of leaving, not from day one. Yes, Maggie was still a piece of work.

As they walked, they talked.

"How long are you staying?"

"I'm staying for as long as I can work. I have to confess, I did call George before I left home, and I asked him if y'all had room for one more."

"I knew it! I knew you called somebody. You're a crazy one, Maggie, but even you aren't crazy enough just to show up with absolutely no plans, and no way of knowing what's next."

Before we talk about work, what did happen with Jimmy? I didn't even know he was sick, or was he?"

'No, it was all kinda sudden. One minute we're eating supper, and the next he's laid out on the floor, clutching his arm and tellin' me to dial 911.

"He had a massive heart attack. It wouldn't have mattered where he was, or what he was doin'; he couldn't have made it. He was gone before the ambulance got there."

As they ate their lunch, they caught up on the issues that Jo and George were tackling at work, and Jo divulged that she was once again in school.

She went to get a teaching degree, a degree she thought at some point she could use. When she finally did tire of working nine to five, she could always teach a few classes online; it would give her something to do, something to fill up her days. And she could teach and talk, when she couldn't do anything else.

George often teased that she just wanted to teach so she could "educate a new generation of cyber warriors, it has nothing to do with filling up your day". There was some truth to what he said. She needed a purpose and a reason to exist. Teaching was better than nothing.

Other than school, and Maggie and George, there was one more thing she began to do sometime towards the end of 2005. She made time for her mom. At least twice a year, she made the trip to check on her mom, and spend some time listening to the latest news in Polk Ridge. She usually kept the visits to weekends, and made no real effort to interact with anyone else at home. Many of the older residents that she remembered from the co-op were long gone, and she had no idea where most of her classmates were. Gina was the only one she knew for sure still lived there, and somehow, Jo just always managed to put off a visit to see her.

Her mom often asked if she wanted to go see Gina, but the weekends were busy; between her errands for her mom, Stella, and Jack, and their three kids, her few days at home were full. So many opportunities to call or visit for just a few minutes, but for Jo, there just never seemed to be enough time.

It wasn't that she didn't think of Gina. She did; in fact, nowadays, she thought about her quite often. Old songs on the radio, or a petite blonde on the street, often reminded her of her old friend.

I know I should make the effort, but my life is still so busy, and what do we really have in common anymore? I'm sure Gina's busy with her life and those two kids. She probably has the same thought I do – too much time has passed.

Elvis was singing "Walk a Mile in my Shoes" on the radio the last time she allowed her mind to travel back in time to revisit her days with Gina, before the military, before she left, when the mountains still held her in their grasp.

George, Maggie, and Jo spent their days as "cyber warriors" and then half the night over drinks as old friends, working to solve their personal dilemmas. George and Jo had never married; Maggie, once married, was now again a single woman. Not one of them had children, and not one of them seemed interested in changing anything about their singular existence. They just enjoyed complaining to each other and as George preferred to say, it was the "highly intelligent and classified lifestyle" that prevented them from marrying; that wasn't, however, the whole truth, especially since Maggie had managed to work a spouse into her "classified" lifestyle.

In truth, George and Jo had never married because neither of them had been willing to compromise any part of their career in order to commit to someone else. Or if there had been a brief moment they were willing, it passed them by before it could become reality.

George Durand was only a year their senior, but had managed to age outwardly, much faster than Maggie and Jo. Of course, they had Miss Clairol, and George did not, nor did he need it. Balding and thin, he wore glasses that made him appear as though he was sixty-ish, rather than the mid-life forty-nine that he actually was. He was also a bit of a loner; the only reason he tolerated Maggie and Jo had more to do with work than social companionship, and he never failed to remind them of that fact.

So, here they sat, at almost the half-century mark, and they had each other and a handful of cyber "geeks" as they were lovingly called at the Department of Defense, to share dinner, drinks, and swap stories that always involved computers and their ability to malfunction, crash, and burn.

Ah, the life of the computers. Jo had spent so many years working with computing from the military standpoint, and then the commercialization opportunities of the "Internet", that the social aspect caught her completely unaware. It was during her last few years in D.C. that she finally became acquainted with Facebook, and the benefits of social media.

Her first encounter with social media was actually Maggie's doing.

"Jo, you seen that new Facebook stuff?"

"No. After I spend all day here at work on a computer, I don't even turn mine on at home."

"Well, you should. It's the latest in socializing. It lets you find old classmates, old friends, even old military friends, just by searching for their name. Then you can post stuff to your page, or message them privately. It's pretty neat."

"You want me to set you up a page? It won't take but a few minutes, and then you can see for yourself--or better yet, come by the apartment and look at mine."

"I just don't care about socializing on my computer, Maggie. I get enough socializing with you and George."

Maggie kept up the barrage, until finally, reluctantly, Jo agreed to come over.

In less than two weeks, Jo had joined the ranks of the Facebook community.

Strange. I spent so many years working on this "Internet" thing and developing a communications network for the military, and I never realized the potential for 'social media;' who knew people would love to connect so much and share such mundane things? I mean, really, who wants to know what I had for supper?

It was also in Washington that she found many of her Air Force Academy classmates, and a few from high school. Paul Collection happened to be one of those "finds."

He had made quite a name for himself in the wine industry, and it was through an Internet ad that she saw an advertisement for "Collection Winery." Suddenly, she was back in high school, on the banks of the Buffalo River, having that final conversation with Paul. Old memories and feelings flooded her mind.

She had found him attractive in a different kind of way; it wasn't that he wasn't attractive, he was. He just wasn't "teenage cute." Looking back, she realized what she had missed at seventeen. The attraction was in the way he carried himself, and in the conversations he had with her. He was self-assured and intelligent, exposed to a world that combined the drinking of wine and the business of making the wine. Paul was years ahead of himself and it had been evident, even as a teenager.

Even at eighteen, he had possessed an astuteness for business, profitability, and marketing. Maybe that was what had drawn her to him in the first place – they had things in common. He worked for his family, just as she did, and he was well-versed in business, just as she had been.

Jo had already had the common sense to be honest with herself, and realized years ago she had loved him then. Maybe something still remained as she clicked to follow the ad to the website. She saw that he had evidently succeeded in the wine industry, since the advertisement and the website spoke of several honors and awards that the Collection Winery had received.

What the hell? It won't hurt to at least "friend" him and say hi. I wonder what he's done with his life besides wine. Does he have a wife? Kids? Only one way to know...

She clicked and sent a request. It would be several months before she received the "acceptance" notice, and then a message. It was just a friendly "glad to hear from you" reply. By then, Jo's thoughts had moved on. She never responded to the message.

Why even bother to try to reconnect? I'm not there, he's not here. And I don't even know what I to say. "Hey Paul, sorry for the pain I caused; sorry I couldn't tell you about my feelings, would you like to be friends?" Yeah, that's really gonna happen.

Her life was a happy place. She just saw no point in revisiting such a painful memory and time for both of them. Living in the nation's capital was an easy and enjoyable time – she loved her work, and she had Maggie and George. As she first reached and then passed her fiftieth birthday, she was happy with her life and her work.

The year that she turned fifty-two, however, something inside her turned a page as well. That gnawing, empty feeling returned. Her mom had passed her seventy-fifth birthday a couple of years ago, and although Stella lived only fifty miles away, it was Jo that Maureen called to solve a problem, ask her opinion, or help her solve a problem. As the last couple of years had passed, so had the frequency of those calls.

Before her dad died, she had seldom talked with her mom; it was with him that she spent long hours sharing her ups and downs and asking his advice. Her mom had always been closer to Stella. Now, it seemed that tide was turning. She wondered if Stella got as many calls as she did. If so, things were worse than she thought.

Maureen still lived in the same house Jo had grown up in. Not much about her life had changed when her dad passed, except that she went to work. She didn't work because she needed to. He had made sure that she didn't need to work, with or without him. Jo suspected she worked because she wanted to be around other people. If she was lonely, she never expressed that fact to Jo.

Her mom had been fairly young when her dad passed, but she had no skills; other than the light bookkeeping she'd done at the co-op, the only other thing she knew how to do was take care of a household.

She didn't call me then, but so much has changed. Maybe she just didn't want to bother me.

Maureen had turned to Gina to help her find some kind of work, and her idea had been a blessing in disguise. It seemed that the Krusty Kup needed a bookkeeper, one that could work for a small hourly wage, and would take a personal interest in the patrons. Maureen accepted the day Melvin made the offer. She liked the conversation and contact that working at the diner brought, and it became an important part of her life. At seventy-five, however, she had decided it was time to give it up and go home. It was time to slow down and spend more time with children and grandchildren. She also began to lean more heavily on Jo.

Maybe it's time to go home. Mom needs me more and more. She's not getting any younger; nor, for that matter, am I. Maybe I need her and Polk Ridge more than I thought.

A few weeks after Jo's fifty-second birthday, she received a short but troublesome call from her mom, and Jo shared her thoughts with George and Maggie over dinner and drinks one Thursday night. It had been a particularly stressful and discouraging day at work. They were lamenting about their age, the stress of their work, and the fact that it might be time to move on.

"Mom called today. It is unbelievable how little she understands about the world around her. Her grasp of technology, and the predators who use that technology, is virtually nonexistent."

"Of course not, Jo. Your mom, and my mom for that matter, grew up in a time when computers and computer technology didn't even exist. By the time they did come along, they were too old to care what a personal computer might do for them, or that someone else might use it to harm them.

My mom's seventy-five. She has no idea how to use an iPhone, let alone a computer. It's still impossible for her to get Internet service, unless it's through the satellite – and I could just see myself trying to explain that process."

It was George that spoke up at this point. "You both should be glad. Try to imagine my life – both my parents are just electronically literate enough to think the government is spying on us – tracking our calls and our texts. You can't imagine the emails I get, the links to this or that 'big brother' website. Dad called the other day to 'alert' me to the fact that this government agency called the 'NSA' is recording his calls--he can tell because of the beeps and noises when he's talking to his buddy in Louisiana. I think he's probably smoked one too many, and he's reached a constant state of paranoia, but hey, what do I know? I'm just some lowly cyber geek working at the Department of Defense."

The revelation brought peals of laughter from the girls.

"Okay, George. Point made. That still doesn't help my mom, or the fact that sooner or later someone's going to take advantage of 'the little old lady on the other end of the phone' and steal her credit, her money, or her assets. I'm thinking it's just about time I return to Polk Ridge, for better or for worse."

And it was Jo that actually posed the next best work alternative: she needed to use that teaching certificate she had. All she had to do was pass the teaching exam that the online schools required, and she could teach from anywhere, so long as she had her computer.

Maggie pressed Jo for more information about working as an online instructor, as George pressed the waitress for another round; as for Jo, she suddenly felt an immense sense of relief.

Have I truly missed home that much? So much so that the mere mention of going home brings such a sense of relief?

She was about to get her answer, because life was going to demand a dramatic change of course.

It was a fall afternoon in D.C. and it was just late enough in the season for the air to feel crisp and cool, making it necessary for a light sweater. The three of them had spent the weekend hiking in Rock Creek Park, and Monday returned to the usual "work, then dinner and drinks" routine.

This Monday night wasn't going to go as planned. Jo had returned to her apartment around 9:30, and upon entering, did her usual: lights on, check the answering machine, pull off socks and shoes, then shower and to bed. Military regimen still played a big role in her daily personal activity. She had considered getting rid of the landline and answering machine, but her mom didn't like talking on the cell, and you could never tell when she might call.

As the answering machine whirred to life, the message that played for her stopped her in mid-sock removal. It was Stella.

"Jo, we're at the hospital and Mom's in surgery. Call me as soon as you get my message." The message was time stamped 5:37 p.m.

She checked her cell phone. She hadn't missed a call from Stella. Why hadn't she called the cell phone? Slightly irritated, and more than a little worried, she pushed the "Stella" contact on her cell phone and waited for her sister to pick up.

As the phone rang and Jo waited for her to answer, she began to run through a mental list of possible problems. What could have happened that she needed surgery? She hadn't seemed sick or out of focus on Friday when she had telephoned to talk with her, before leaving to go hiking. What could have possibly happened so quickly?

It would be the following morning before she got an answer. Stella's voicemail picked up, and although Jo wasn't happy about leaving a message, what choice did she really have? The original message hadn't given a hospital, or another contact number, or any real details that helped her locate her mom.

She spent a rather sleepless night imagining all sorts of terrible situations and possibilities, and it wasn't until her phone rang in the kitchen that she even realized that she had fallen asleep. She sprang to life at the sound of the phone ringing and raced to get to it before the answering machine picked up.

"Hello?"

"Jo! Hey, it's me. Did you get my message last night?"

"Yeah, I got it. Why didn't you call my cell? I could've caught a plane home last night, but I didn't know where to go, and I didn't get your message 'til 9:30. What happened?"

"Well, it seems she's been havin' these dizzy spells, and yesterday mornin' it was so bad that she fell tryin' to get to the kitchen. She broke her leg. Thank God it wasn't her hip; you know how hard that can be on someone Momma's age." *Get on with it, Stella. Skip the personal opinions.* "Anyway, Gina found her, called the ambulance, and then called me. We're in Flowood. Is there anywhere else to go? Room 218. I've got my phone with me. Just call it instead of the hospital phone. Are you coming today?"

Unable to get up and get to her phone, it was Monday afternoon before Gina found her. She had tried to call Maureen all morning, to no avail. Worried, and unable to get Stella on the phone, she drove over to check on Maureen when she finished her volunteer activities at the Family Services Center. It was Gina that called the ambulance and finally managed to get Stella to let her know they were on their way to Flowood with Maureen. Stella and Jack got there around 5:30 p.m., and it was at that point that she left Jo a message.

Jo caught the first flight available from Washington to Little Rock, and arrived on Wednesday morning. The flight and the trip were exhausting, but the situation that confronted her when she arrived in Polk Ridge was even more draining. At seventy-two, Maureen was still in pretty good health, but the broken leg and the ensuing surgery had thrown the old lady off her game. She was awake, but she hadn't regained all of her senses, often confusing her daughters in the first few days of recovery. Jo stayed with her mom on Wednesday night and Stella returned to take Thursday's watch.

When Jo finally made it to her childhood home, it was an even more disconcerting scene. The usually spotless house was a disorderly scene.

What was Momma thinking? Or was she thinking?

Dirty dishes covered the kitchen counter. Laundry of all stages littered the living room, and Maureen's bedroom was a complete wreck. It was then that she realized it *really* was time to come home. She had lived too far away, for far too long. Mentally, she began to make plans to return to Polk Ridge. It was time to come home.

Less than two months after Maureen's accident, Jo had turned in her notice in D.C., found a position with an online university as an instructor, and made preparations to return home. There was just one small problem: she didn't want to move in with her mom. She just wanted to be closer, and housing in Polk Ridge wasn't the easiest thing to find.

In such a small community, renting an apartment was a nearly non-existent option, and she didn't want to rent a house. She needed to find something to buy. But what, and where? The answer surprised her in more ways than one.

Before she left D.C., she decided to check out the real estate websites around Polk Ridge. Surely, there was something for sale that she could buy. Finally, after several days of searching, she came across Buffalo River Rental Properties. The pictures she saw were of quaint cabins, located in and around the Buffalo River. There was one that was only a few miles from her mom's place.

Maybe I should just rent one of these for a couple of months. It's the off season, and I'm sure it would be available long enough for me to find something.

She took down the number and dialed her cell phone. An answering machine picked up, so she just left her name and number. No sense going into detail with a machine. Surely they would call her back in a couple of days.

Later in the week, she still hadn't heard from the Rental Properties. *I'll just give 'em one more call.*

She dialed the number again.

"Hello, Buffalo River Rental Properties."

"Yes, ma'am. I am interested in one of your cabins, but I need to rent a place for several months, not just a week or two. Is that possible?"

"Well, I don't know. We've never rented 'em for more than a couple of weeks at a time. Let me have someone call you back. Is this a good number to reach you around 6?"

"Yes, that will be fine. It's my cell. My name is Jo Felsenthal."

She spent the rest of her afternoon waiting on the call.

Her phone rang at exactly 6.

"Jo?"

She didn't immediately recognize the voice on the other end.

"Yes, this is Jo."

"It's Paul. You called about the cabins?"

She suddenly recognized the voice on the other end. Paul Collections. Surprise was evident in her voice.

"Those are yours?"

"Yeah, we built those mostly for an investment, but it's always nice to have someplace to go stay on the river during the summer. Why do you need a cabin? Where are you now?"

"I'm coming home. Mom broke her leg a few months ago, and she doesn't seem to be doin' all that good. It's just time for me to come home, and I need a place to live. I found the cabins on the Internet, and there's one that's only a few miles from Mom. I need to be kinda close to her."

"Give me your email address, and I'll forward the information to you. We should be able to take care of you, no matter which cabin you want."

They talked for another half hour about her mom, his business, anything that kept them away from what they wanted to ask. As Jo began to say her goodbye and hang up, Paul interrupted her. "Jo, it'll be good to see you. And I'm glad you finally decided to come home."

When she checked her email the next morning, there was the information he had promised. What she didn't expect, however, was the offer he made her in the email. He sent photos of all the cabins, and told her to pick the one she wanted. It was hers until she had time to decide what she wanted to do permanently. He had to be in California for the next several months and included his cell phone number, with instructions to call if she needed anything. He had signed it with:

Welcome Home, Major Felsenthal

Paul

CHAPTER 10

Wednesday, May 19, 2012

GINA GATHERED HER PURSE, keys, and cell phone. It was time. She went out the kitchen door, closed and locked it, and got in the car.

Will Jo be excited to see me? Will the years roll away? Damn! I forgot the yearbook. Ah, just go back and get it, Gina. If things aren't the same between you two, at least you'll have something to talk about.

After retrieving the yearbook, she started the car and pulled out. Jo's cabin was only a short distance, but it seemed almost an eternity to Gina. Twenty minutes later, she turned down her drive.

I'm here. I'm really here. And I'm really nervous.

Gina's shoes made no sound as she moved from her car to the front door. All she heard was the thud of her heart. Excitement and dread filled her simultaneously. Would the years roll away with the opening of the front door? A sinking feeling of apprehension made her want to turn and run, but her need to fill the void of closeness and familiarity with her old friend steadied her gait toward the front door. Whatever the outcome, the moment of truth was at hand. She rang the bell.

The door opened. They finally stood just feet apart, with long years of separation between them.

"Hi, old friend." Gina smiled, just a little misty-eyed at the sight of Jo.

"Hello. My God, it's been a long, long time. C'mon in, let's see if we can pick up some of the pieces; it can't be that hard to find our way back. I fixed coffee, but I didn't have a clue as to how you drink it, or if you drink it. Want a cup?" Jo's smile was still the same.

"I do drink it, and as of late, I take my cream and sugar with coffee. Gotta watch the caffeine. I don't want to be up all night! Do you think we could still manage to sit up all night and talk about the last forty years, like we used to talk about the boys and the plans we had?"

Before Jo could answer, Gina was talking again.

"Thank you for accepting my Facebook invite. I almost swallowed my tongue when I searched for you and found out that you were in the Polk Ridge area again. Why didn't you call? I couldn't wait to see you and talk with you. It's been such a long time, and we have so much to catch up on. I can only visit a few hours today. I've got to spend the afternoon with a young woman that I work with in my volunteer role at the North Arkansas Ozark Family Services Center. But I can't wait to hear about what you've done, where you've been, and what you're doing now."

"Hey, wasn't that my line?" asked Jo.

They shared a laugh, and some of the old camaraderie returned.

They were still standing in the doorway. It seemed as though some things would never change.

The two women made their way to the kitchen, talking the entire time – sometimes to each other, sometimes over each other, but with the same closeness they had known so many years earlier.

Once seated at the kitchen table, the conversation flowed almost endlessly. There were so many questions they needed to ask each other. They weren't sure where to start, so they simply started.

"I'm just a little put out with you, Jorja Felsenthal. How long have you been back? Why didn't you call? I haven't even seen you in town or talked to anybody that told me you were back. Whatcha been doin', hidin' out over here?"

"Yeah, I guess I have. I got back right after Christmas, and between trying to setup for work and dealing with my mom, I haven't tried to visit anybody – hell, I haven't been to town, except to buy gas for the Jeep. I order most of my groceries online – I have developed an aversion to shopping – and there's not a lot of choice up here anyway."

"Well, at least we have a Wal-Mart now. It took us 'til '98 to get that."

"Yeah, I visited one of those. I made the mistake of going to one in Muscle Shoals with Maggie one time—too many people and too many lines. No thanks! I'd rather order online and wait on UPS. I do use Wal-Mart's online shopping option, though. The only thing you can't get online is frozen or refrigerated stuff, so I usually get freeze-dried or canned. It keeps me from visiting the store."

"I can't imagine life without Wally World. They don't have them in D.C., do they?"

"No, not yet. The unions don't want them. Speaking of unions, I've got to find out if I have to join the teachers union in Arkansas or Nevada. I got my teaching certificate for Arkansas before I left D.C., but I'm working for the University of Phoenix, and they're based in Nevada."

"You're teaching?"

"Yes, online classes. I went back to school while I was in Washington and got my certificate. I wanted to have something that would complement my network security skills, no matter where I found myself living. And it's a good thing I did – especially with mom's situation."

"Oh, yeah – how is Miss Maureen doin'? I haven't talked with her much since she fell. I figured Stella was still comin' down to see about her."

"She's doin' alright, but I couldn't believe that house when I got there the day after the accident. It was a wreck. You found her, didn't you? What did you think?"

"Yes, I did, but to be honest, I didn't even look at the house after I found her," said Gina.

"I guess I didn't realize how quickly Mom was declining until she broke her leg. It was as if she no longer cared if the dishes were done, if the laundry was folded, or if the floors were swept. I wasn't sure I was walking into the right house. It was then that I figured it was time to come home. She needed me more than I needed to stay in Washington."

"I think she's been experiencing some sort of depression," continued Jo. "I know since giving up work she hasn't had much to fill her days, and I suppose I could have come home more often, but you just don't think about your parents experiencing issues such as depression when your life is busy and hectic. Their daily life is not yours."

Gina sighed. "You're right. My dad has never fully gotten over losing my mom even though it was so many years ago. He stays active, and involved in the community, but he just doesn't have that spark and drive that he had when mom was around.

"You know, he came to Robert and I about a year after Mom passed and wanted to give us the house," continued Gina. "He couldn't bear all the memories that every room held. He moved into the rental house Robert and I had and we moved into the house I grew up in. I didn't really realize until then how lonely he must have been. He's now almost to the point that I think he really needs to be in an assisted living facility." She paused with her thoughts.

"I just haven't had the heart to approach him with the idea. He loves the freedom that old truck gives him and he hasn't been a danger to anyone, yet."

"Speaking of danger, my coffee cup is dangerously low. How about you? You need a refill?"

Jo got up and refilled their cups. As she made her way across the kitchen, Gina's eyes took in the surroundings of the small cabin.

It was made out of real logs inside and out. The furnishings were sparse but efficient, and Jo littered the adjoining living room with all sorts of electronics – a computer and printer, an Internet Wi-Fi box, an iPod stereo and speakers, and some sort of strange, black box labeled "Department of Defense." The only thing that looked out of place among all the electronics was the huge stack of worn books in the corner by the couch.

I wonder what those are, Gina thought.

"I see your housekeeping skills are still the same. You never did mind clutter. What is all this electronic stuff for? It resembles an FBI setup."

She giggled that same girlish giggle from her youth.

"Yeah, right – I'm working for the NSA."

At that, Gina gave her a blank stare.

"Who?"

"Never mind, it's something George and I kept up as a running joke."

"Who's George? Are you two dating?"

"Heavens, no. George is a loner from hell. I don't think there's a woman on this planet that could date George. He's just a friend, and I worked with him. He's a cyber-geek, too."

"Alright, if you're not dating George, who are you dating? I know you're not married, because of your Facebook status."

"Nobody. Honestly, Gina, it's just such a hassle. I tried several times, while I was in D.C., but between my work, and then spending time with Maggie and George, it just never worked out."

"Now, who's Maggie? That's the second time you've mentioned Maggie, so who is she?"

"She's a friend from the Air Force Academy," said Jo. "We were roommates, and then when we were commissioned, we remained friends. We both went to France, and then we were together in a few other places. She is a piece of work. I hope you get to meet her. She's from Muscle Shoals, Alabama, and loves the mountains just as much as we do."

"Okay, if you're not dating anybody now, did you ever slow down long enough to meet *anybody* in all this traveling and living life?"

"Before I answer that, let me answer your question about all of this electronic equipment. I'm teaching online classes--I think I already mentioned that. Anyway, I need all of this equipment in order to access the Internet and email with my students. I am amazed at the lack of Internet service around here. Do you have DSL or Wi-Fi at home? I don't want to use the satellite service. It's horrible, but I haven't found any cable or telephone company that offers DSL."

"Yeah, I have AT&T DSL at home, but you won't be able to get it up here. You have to live pretty close to town to get that. Do you enjoy the teaching?"

"Yes, I do, but not as much as my work in D.C."

"What exactly did you do in the Air Force? Maureen tried to explain it to me once, but I just couldn't understand what she was talking about."

Jo gave her a half grin. "That's because she doesn't understand it either."

At that point, Jo explained the more intricate details of her position as a network security team leader. She began with the way a team is put together then moved on to the role that each team member plays in establishing effective communication and security protocols.

Gina stopped her only once. That was when Jo tried to explain about establishing protocols, packet switching, and network relays.

"Jo," she interjected, "there's no point in explaining all that stuff in detail. I have trouble with a mouse and a keyboard, never mind all the finite behind-the-scenes pieces. I won't understand it even if you explained that process ten times over."

She giggled again. "Just like Miss Maureen. But I do understand that makes you an extremely smart woman!"

When Gina said "smart," Jo's mind brought Phillip into sharp focus and she recalled the question Gina had asked earlier.

"Well, there is one other part of my life that I need to share with you, and his name is Phillip Smart—Brigadier General Phillip Smart, to be exact."

Jo took a deep breath and began to recount her heartache and loss.

"I sometimes wonder if it was a blessing or a curse that we never returned to one another. I can see now that I might have given up a very promising career all for the sake of being with him. And I can also see now that maybe it wasn't the best thing for me. Nonetheless, what I felt was an emotion so powerful that I can definitely understand the old saying, 'It is better to have loved and lost than never to have loved at all.'"

Gina responded in a low, and somewhat saddened tone, "You know, when you start life, you never see the snags, pitfalls, or opportunities for catastrophe. You expect life to be one smooth highway for the entire journey, and that is so far from reality. What you eventually realize is that you're collecting unique memories of a journey, whether it's a winding road or the straight and narrow, you look back on the life you've lived, and it resembles one of those old scrapbooks my mom made. Full of faded pictures, torn and frayed around the edges, but overflowing with memories—good and bad."

Each woman was quiet for a few minutes. Jo thought about Phillip Smart, and Gina thought about Robert. Gina finally broke the silence.

"And, speaking of scrapbooks, I brought our class yearbook. I thought we might wanna look back so I can catch you up on all our classmates. I've found a lot of them on Facebook."

"Oh, no, I don't know if I can take a walk down that memory lane. The hair, the clothes… what were we thinking?"

As they turned the pages, the two women relived the memories of their youth. Their hair *was* unbelievable. The clothes were even worse. But Gina caught Jo up to date on everyone except Paul Collections and Robert Phillips.

"Do you want to tell me about Robert? I know it's gotta be hard, and if you'd rather wait 'til another time, that's fine. When my mom told me what had happened, I couldn't believe he was gone. You just don't think about losing someone your own age so soon."

"No," Gina replied. "It's best to go ahead and deal with life straight up. I've learned that, too, over all these years. You and I need to be able to talk about all the things that have happened over our lifetimes, and this is part of my life. The hard part is that I am never really prepared to talk about him in the past tense. It almost seems as if it happened in another life."

Gina spent the next hour talking about Robert's accident, the weeks and months that followed, and how she returned to school. She included Melvin in the conversation but was hesitant to share more than she needed to about Melvin's role in her life. She really wasn't ready to talk about that part of her life with Jo – not just yet.

"For so many weeks after the accident, I couldn't even get out of bed, let alone function as a mom and a person. It was your mom that forced me to snap out of my depression and remember that I had two children who desperately needed their mother."

"I'm so sorry you didn't have your own mother to talk to," said Jo. "I know you weren't that close, but she was a strong person, and she would've been able to help you. I can't imagine what it must have been like to lose her, but when I lost my dad, I began to think about you during those early years. How old were you when she passed?"

"Twenty-four, and no, you can't imagine how lost I felt. I mean, really, as an only child, I had no idea about babies and diapers, and burping and bottles. If it hadn't been for her, I can't imagine what kind of childhood Jax and Millie might have had." Gina smiled in a melancholy way.

"She and I were the closest we had ever been when all that happened. For several weeks after her passing, all I could do was feel sorry for myself. I had lost you to the Air Force, and now I had lost my mom to death. I felt hurt, angry, and resentful. That's when your mom helped me to see that life is always going to throw you curveballs, it's how you deal with them that defines you as a person, and defines the happiness you find in life."

Gina continued, "I can never repay Maureen for the kindness and lessons she helped to teach me during that time in my life, and that's why I've continued to stay close to her all these years. That, and the fact that she always managed to keep me updated on Jo's travels!"

Gina smiled out of genuine happiness at her old friend. She felt inside as though a piece of the puzzle had been returned to its rightful place, right across the table.

Jo responded with the same kind of smile. She, too, felt as if something that had been missing had suddenly reappeared to complete a picture.

"So, Jax and Millie never really got to know your mom?"

How sad, Jo thought. *Louise had been a great person, and she knew she would have been a great grandmother.*

"No," Gina replied, "but they never really lacked for grandmothers. Thanks to your mom, Robert's mom, and their great-grandparents on Robert's side of the family, they had more than enough attention. They were great kids to raise. I enjoyed every minute. Robert was a great dad, and we were fortunate to have them and each other."

Gina paused.

"I suppose you felt the same way when you lost your dad?"

"Yes, it was one of the hardest things I've ever experienced," said Jo. "He was my dad, but as I got older, he was also my friend. In fact, during those first few years in the military, he was the only best friend I had. In the beginning, I wrote him letters. Then as time passed, we'd talk on the phone at least once a week about military life, difficult job assignments, and the stress of working sometimes ten- or twelve-hour days. He tried really hard to understand exactly what it was that I did in my work, and no one has ever come close to the effort he gave to encourage me.

"When I got that phone call from Stella," Jo continued, "I felt as if the rug had been pulled out from under me. I was so far away and likely not to make it back in time to say goodbye. The fact that I did still amazes me today. I believe he waited until I got there.

"Then there were all the arrangements and my mom and Stella's inability to agree. I felt as if the threads of our family were torn into shreds. It was the hardest thing I've ever faced.

"But you know, when I'm feeling particularly low, and life throws something at me that I just don't think I can deal with, I hear my dad's voice and the advice that he gave so often: *Jo, it's always darkest before the dawn.* It's amazing that I can still clearly hear him and the memories that play in my mind still bring me comfort."

"That's true, Jo. I experience the same thing with the memories of my mom. We collect those memories, and when we need them, they're there, regardless of the time that has passed or the circumstances that exist."

"Speaking of Stella," continued Gina, "I know that you two aren't that close, but how is she? I rarely ever hear your mom mention her and Jack, but she talks about her grandsons, Austin, Ethan and Hagen, all the time. Just not very much about Stella and Jack."

Jo hadn't thought about that. Gina was right, of course. Jo and Stella weren't that close. There was a large age gap between them, and they were two totally different people.

Stella Felsenthal married Jack Gentle in 1969, the summer she graduated from high school and Jo was in fourth grade. Jo was fond of Jack, and when he and Stella dated, he was kind and attentive to a ten-year-old Jo.

Once married, they moved to a town in Missouri just north of the Arkansas-Missouri state line. He took a job in Branson as a car salesman, and she ran the household and was a part-time backup singer in a music studio. They didn't have children until they were well into their thirties, and then it was like opening a faucet and three boys were born in less than ten years.

Jack often worked on Saturday and most holidays, so the visits with Tom, Maureen, and Jo were sparse at best, and this was especially true once the boys arrived.

"Well, I don't talk to my sister very much," said Jo. "I know that Jack still works at a Ford dealership, and she's never worked outside the home other than the part-time work she did as a backup singer. Can you believe she could sing? The boys are almost grown. Austin is twenty-four and finishing his last year of college – you know he's a great athlete and went to college on a baseball scholarship. Ethan is nineteen and a freshman in college. He works as a musician in Branson. I'm sure Stella helped him get that job. Hagen is only fourteen. I don't think he knows what he wants to do yet, other than escaping his mother's attention and playing junior league soccer and his video games."

They both laughed. Stella could be quite a dominating person. As Tom had once remarked, *"Poor Jack doesn't stand a chance, Stella probably tells him what to do twenty-four, seven!"*

"You know, there is one thing about my sister that amazes me. She has stood beside Jack through every crazy idea and plan that the poor man has had. The first one came along when I was probably sixteen, and that was the idea he had to invest in a customized T-shirt shop, then there was the 'mood rings' that he spent several thousand dollars on… and there's more. I just quit keeping track."

"She's supported all of those dreams and never once complained that it was a waste of time or money," continued Jo. "I know she's bossy, and I know she's demanding, but she's a true believer in Jack. I've never been able to do that. I think he finally got it right with the video arcade they opened in a mall in Branson during '89. Dad used to say that if Jack ever found the right dream, he and Stella should be able to make it work. Lord knows they've had enough practice!"

"And I'm not sure what's happened between Mom and Stella, but something has changed. I guess that will be something I'll hear about from one or the other, sooner or later. Oh, and speaking of kids, what about your two? Where are Jax and Millie, and what are they doing now?"

"Well, Jax is in Little Rock. He got a degree in finance, and he's working for an accounting firm. He's been dating a girl he met in college, Vicky Sudduth, but he doesn't seem the least bit inclined to marry her. Now Millie, on the other hand, got married right out of college."

"What did she get her degree in, and where did she go?"

"MSU, in Starkville, Mississippi--and she's a conservationist. She has a degree in environmental management. I swear, I believe she loves these mountains more than she loves me!"

"Anyway, as I said, she married right out of college and came back here to the Buffalo River National Park for work. She married a young man named David White from Huntsville, Alabama. She's got two little girls, Henley Jane and Bella Kate. They're twins--not identical, though--and it shows. They each have their own personality, and both are blonde with blue eyes, just like me. They're in the second grade. I really worried that they inherited my dyslexia, but neither of them have any trouble with reading and writing their letters so far. They call me 'Ginny.' I guess they put 'granny' and 'Gina' together. One wants to be a vet, and the other is enrolled in tumbling and cheering classes… I don't know where she gets that from." Gina smiled that same old mischievous smile.

"Yeah, right. I bet you don't," said Jo. "I could never understand why you liked that so much, and I still don't today… but what the heck? I guess you didn't understand why I liked to read so much either. But I can tell you one thing I do understand: how special those years we shared were to me, and how much I've missed your company."

At that, Gina let out one of those famous giggles. "Well, we're not dead yet. There's still lots of time to make more memories. I've got a bucket list of ideas, and I am in sore need of a partner. How about it, Miss Air Force lady? Wanna try your hand at Polk Ridge again?"

At that, they laughed and reminisced further. Patched, battered, and torn, it looked like they might have room for one more journey.

"What exactly do you have on the list, and how dangerous might this be to my mental or physical health?" Jo asked, as she refilled their coffee for the fourth time.

"Well," Gina began, "I've spent most of my life being a mom, a wife, and working either at home or at the Center. I think it's about time I spent some time doing the things I've wanted to do but pushed to the back of my mind because of other obligations. For instance, I want to hike every trail in the Buffalo River National Park; I want to visit the beach – a real beach on a real ocean – and I wanna jump from an airplane."

Jo simply stared at her friend as she spoke. "Beaches and hiking I can do, but jumping from an airplane? Are you crazy? We could get killed! I knew at least one idea of ours was going to endanger me mentally, emotionally, or physically!"

"Jo," Gina retorted, "we could get killed driving a car. If it's time for me to go, I wanna be doing something I enjoy and have never experienced. But don't worry, we can save the airplane thing for last."

Wednesday morning's conversation covered much ground, but the two women had barely scratched the surface; there was still Polk Ridge news to share, Gina's work at the center, and most importantly, plans for the future. Tomorrow was the land of opportunity for these two—all sorts of opportunities.

When they looked at the clock for the first time since they began their conversation, it was 12:20 p.m. Both women were taken aback – could it be possible that they had talked for almost four hours?

"Oh my goodness," Gina exclaimed. "I've got to move now if I'm gonna make my afternoon appointment!"

Then she looked at Jo with that impish grin and asked, "Whatcha doin' tomorrow?"

CHAPTER 11

JO MAY HAVE RETIRED from the military, but the military training hadn't retired from Jo. This was especially true when she woke up in the morning. She was up at 5 a.m. every day regardless of the day's planned events, and this morning was no different.

It was with some excitement that she greeted the day, wandered to the kitchen, and retrieved the morning's first cup of coffee. She had enjoyed Gina's visit more than she could say, and when it came time for her to leave yesterday, Jo really wasn't ready to suspend the conversation.

When Gina asked if she wanted to join her for coffee at the Krusty Kup the next day, she had enthusiastically agreed and today she looked forward to the 9 a.m. rendezvous.

She had taken comfort from her old friend's smile the day before, and like a child in the sunshine, she was ready to soak up some more.

Yesterday, Gina bid Jo goodbye and sped off in the Volkswagen to make her 1 p.m. appointment at the Center. She had been so apprehensive about her meeting with Jo, and it was all for nothing. It had seemed as if thirty-plus years of separation had rolled away as quickly as the time during their visit.

She had missed Jo more than she realized. When she finally roused herself from sleep, it was already 7:45 a.m., and she would have to hurry to make it to the Krusty Kup by 9. But make it she would; she wasn't about to miss the opportunity to continue their conversation.

Gina spent at least two or three mornings a week at the Krusty Kup for two reasons: one, she really enjoyed talking with some of the locals, and two, because of Melvin. He was always there and had been a friend and shoulder to lean on when she lost Robert.

Just a day earlier, she hadn't been ready to share the more intimate details of her relationship with Melvin, but after the conversation and closeness she shared with Jo the day before, and the fact that Jo revealed so much about her romance with Phillip, Gina decided it might be time.

Besides, Jo's not blind.. She'll pickup on the closeness we share within a few short minutes, and it might hurt her feelings if I don't confide about him, especially because she was so open with me.

When Gina got to the Krusty Kup, Jo's vehicle was already in the parking lot. She smiled to herself.

She's just as glad to see me as I am to see her.

As she entered the diner, she spotted Jo seated with a couple of the locals, and she plopped down at the already crowded table.

"Good morning, everyone! Looks like we're having a reunion and you guys started without me!" Gina laughed and proceeded to jump right into the conversation.

Jo, almost as comfortable with Gina now as she had been years earlier, said, "You're late, and I was early, so I struck up a conversation with these folks I haven't seen in years. I'm so glad I decided to meet you here today. I get a chance to catch up on all the happenings here over the last several decades. And we're just gettin' started."

They visited with the other women until almost 10 a.m., and then they all began to disperse; appointments and prior responsibilities dictating their departure, allowing Jo and Gina to pick up where they left off the day before.

"Gina, how do you have the energy to volunteer, babysit, take care of a home, and still act like you're ready for the Boston Marathon? I'm exhausted just contemplating it."

"Testosterone, baby. Testosterone. I go get my implants like clockwork."

"You seriously go get testosterone implants? Do you realize the consequences to your health? Is it good for you? What does it do to your heart?"

Gina's face was a crumpled cross between disdain and disbelief.

"Of course I checked it out, and there are some risks, but I don't wanna feel like shit every day, Jo. I'd rather go out with a bang than drag myself to the edge and fall off. We're all gonna die one day anyway, so why not have loads of energy while you're here? Besides, there aren't any real bad side effects. Not that I've seen yet."

"You sound like a commercial for cocaine. You realize that, don't you?"

"No, I don't. I sound like a woman with a mission, and I want to feel good on my mission. Did you eat breakfast yet? I didn't, and I'm starved. Heck, it's almost lunch. Where's Melvin?"

Gina strode off in the direction of the kitchen, returning shortly with a plate of home-fried potatoes, an omelet, and a pile of hash browns.

"Do you know what waitresses are for, Gina?"

"Yes," she giggled, "but when you're best friends with the owner, you don't have to wait on the waitress. Now, back to your question about energy. It's all in the conditioning. I still love hiking in the Ozarks, I try to meditate every day, and I've managed to stay in shape. Most days, I can conquer the world." She giggled again. "Well, if not the world, at least Polk Ridge! Speaking of which, you seem pretty healthy yourself, Jo. What do you do? Snort cocaine?"

"No, ass. I still go hiking, too. Granted, I'm not *taking* anything, but I still feel pretty good, and when I was in Washington, I went to the range to target practice. Maybe not as interesting as hiking, but it's great for relieving stress."

"You never told me much about your time in Washington yesterday," said Gina. "Once you retired from the military, why did you decide to go to Washington?"

"Well, I wasn't ready to return to Polk Ridge. Really, I wasn't even sure if I wanted to. I also wasn't ready to completely retire, and George was already working in Washington as a contractor with the Department of Defense. Cyber warfare was on the upswing, and as a country, we weren't as prepared as we needed to be to deal with the outside threats from countries like China and Russia. So I gave George a call, and he set it up for me to talk to the company he was working for, and then I spent the next ten or so years working for the Department of Defense."

"Wow, and I thought I had an interesting job. No wonder you were so hesitant to return here – we don't get a lot of cyber-anything up here," she chuckled. "About the only cyber experience I know exists in the kids' video games."

Gina launched into a conversation about the huge differences in childhood experiences that existed between her and Jo versus her grandchildren.

"The technology that exists today was something we couldn't even dream about. Sometimes, I'm completely lost when my grandkids talk about Wi-Fi and game apps they want me to download on my phone, although I have found an Elvis app that I got one of the girls at work to download."

She stopped long enough to share a smile with Jo.

"Oh no," Jo groaned. "You aren't still infatuated with the Elvis stuff, are you? Do you still have a shrine in your house like you had when you were a teenager?"

"Absolutely," Gina replied. "Besides Robert, he's the only man who ever stole my heart. And… well, now Melvin."

There—she said it out loud, and perhaps for the first time ever to anyone, even her family or friends. Jo's mouth flew open.

"This Melvin?" she squeaked.

"This Melvin."

"No wonder you come to the Krusty Kup so much," Jo teased. "And here I thought it was the 'great conversation and coffee' that kept you coming back! Okay. Spill it." Jo demanded. "I want details!"

They spent the next hour talking in hushed voices as Gina shared about Melvin's role in her life: how she had turned to him to help with financial decisions, and then later about returning to school. Somewhere along the way, Melvin filled the need for companionship that was so sorely missing in her life. Finally, exhausted from talking, Gina paused to rest while Jo soaked up the unbelievable information.

She's dating Melvin—Melvin from Dairy Queen. Wow.

The two were silent for several minutes.

Gina finally broke the silence. "Why don't we plan a hike this weekend? Are you doing anything else? I know it's kind of early in the season, but it's beautiful up there, and it really is great for stress. C'mon, what do you say?"

She thought about it for a few minutes. Jo really didn't have anything planned for the weekend, and it had been a while since she'd even thought about hiking and exploring the Ozarks. She had truly enjoyed their treks through the mountains as a young girl.

"Okay. What time do you want to leave Saturday, and how long is this hike going to take?" she asked.

"Well, let's just do something simple for you because you haven't been in a while, and we only have a couple of days. How about we leave your cabin by 6 a.m. and hike the Lost Valley Trail. It only takes a couple of hours and isn't that hard. Then, if you're up to it, we could visit my friends at the store up there Saturday afternoon. Oh yeah, and we could zip line on Sunday once we've finished hiking!"

"Zip lining? Seriously, Gina, isn't the hike enough?"

Although Jo was in great shape, she wasn't too sure she wanted to pick up zip lining, under any conditions.

Gina erupted in that famous giggle. "You'll love it! I've already been several times. The view is unbelievable, and the time you spend flying over the trees is indescribable! You've got to try it at least once!"

Jo reluctantly agreed to take a look at the zip line, but she wasn't promising her old friend any participation—just a look. She couldn't wait to revisit the Buffalo River National Park and hike the beautiful trails, so they agreed to meet Saturday morning at 6 a.m. at Jo's cabin and spend Saturday and Sunday in nature and reminiscing about the past.

"Oh, and one more thing, Jo," Gina began. "My friends that I want you to meet are mostly retired and have their own little community up there. There's Max and Maxine, Aaron, Lucy, Bob, and some guy named Paul--I haven't met him yet. I think you'll really enjoy meeting all of them, and of course, they have a store – so if we need anything, we can grab it Saturday afternoon."

"Okay, as long as you promise I won't die on the zip line or the hiking trail, it's a date," said Jo. "For now, I gotta go. I've got an on-line class I am scheduled to teach at 1 p.m., and I'm starving. By the way, thanks for the invitation this morning. I really have enjoyed the atmosphere of the Krusty Kup and the chance to see some folks I haven't seen in years."

"Yes. I really love coming here several mornings during the week just to spend time with people. It's something to look forward to, and besides…" Gina lowered her voice and looked around to make sure no one was listening. "I catch all the latest gossip just by listening to all these old women talk – I don't have to say one word, and I know what is happening in Polk Ridge social clubs, police department, at the high school, everything."

"Gina," Jo retorted, her eyes wide with a smile on her lips, "we *are* these old women, and I don't believe for one second you have nothing to contribute to the conversation – you never let an opportunity to talk pass you by! And speaking of old women, I see some gray in that blonde hair."

"No, you don't, do you? Damn, I forgot it was time to get the Miss Clairol out. I forgot to write it on my calendar, and I knew I'd slip up and let the gray show."

"You too, huh? I've told George a hundred times, as long as they make Miss Clairol 129, My hair will be auburn 'til I die!"

Both women burst into laughter, picked up their purses and made their way to the door. Jo to teach her class, and Gina to greet her grandkids as they got off the bus to spend the afternoon at Ginny's.

As Friday morning made its way into each woman's life, there were houses to clean, errands to run, and parents to check on. And that was the easy part.

Gina woke up that Friday morning to a ringing phone, and her dad's voice on the other end. Floyd Ingram normally rose early and went to the Krusty Kup to eat breakfast and visit with the other "old-timers" in town. She often teased her father that old men could gossip more than any bunch of women.

This Friday started out no differently, but by 7 a.m., he had hit a snag.

"Gina," he bellowed. "Can you come down here to the house? Some damn kid slammed into the back of my truck. The cops are here, but they need insurance information, and I can't find my card. It ain't in the truck. Can you come?"

"Dad, are you all right? Did it hurt you?"

"Aw, yeah, I'm fine. These kids just fly through here. They don't watch where they're goin' and don't give you time to get out of the way even if you wanted to."

Really? There's at least a hundred yards of street, and he didn't see a car coming?

And that was just the beginning.

On the other end of Polk Ridge, Jo rose at her customary 5 a.m. and saw that she had a text message. It was George. "Call me ASAP" was all it read, but he'd already sent it three times.

This can't be good, she thought.

She called George after grabbing a cup of coffee.

"Hey," the voice on the other end greeted. "I need your help really, really badly."

"Well, good morning, George. How are you? I'm fine. Thanks for asking."

"Sorry, Jo. But this is bad. No time for all that nice stuff."

As each woman moved throughout their daily routine, they thought about each other and their renewed friendship. It was their bright spot in a day filled with responsibilities, unplanned events, and the stress of coping.

That night, Gina ended the rollercoaster of events with a hot bath and Elvis on her stereo.

Thank God today is over. I can't wait 'til tomorrow. This week has been a ride.

Jo sat on her front porch, soaking up the final rays of sun just before it dipped below the mountaintop. As it slowly slipped from her view, she extinguished the last cigarette of the day and went inside.

What a week! I've not been so exhausted since I left the military. It must be an emotional thing. Seeing Gina brought back so many memories.

She had high hopes for a weekend that would bring some rest and more catch up conversation with Gina.

She had no idea what awaited them in the Ozarks for the weekend, and for that matter, neither did Gina.

You can't always get what you want...

AUTHOR AND WRITER, NATALIE R VICE has spent a lifetime preparing for the stories created in *The Scrapbook Series.* A collection of stories focused on the lives of Jo and Gina, two women raised in the Ozark Mountains of northern Arkansas. She draws upon her life experiences as a young woman raised in small town America for the funny and sometimes dysfunctional adventures of the characters as they come together for the pursuit of lost friendship and new adventures.

Born in 1965, on an Air Force Base, her parents returned to the small town way of life to live and raise their 3 children. Natalie has spent most of her life within a 50 mile radius of that same small town, observing and finding humor in the everyday "mishaps" that occur when life is lived in a small town.

She has been an author, blogger and freelance writer for well over a decade and holds a Bachelor of Science in Accounting. In addition to creating *The Scrapbook Series,* she also offers services for the business, finance and education industries.

In 1977, at the TG&Y in Fayette, Al, I bought a plaque of an old Irish proverb/prayer. One of those lines reads:

Take time to dream, it is hitching your wagon to a star.

I still have the plaque; it hangs on my office wall and I still take time to dream. In following the dream of writing, I created the characters of Jorja Felsenthal and Regina Ingram and began their story.

THE SCRAPBOOK SERIES IS an opportunity to look at life through the eyes of the most unsung hero in American life: the everyday, average woman. We take life as it comes and find a way to deal with unbelievable situations: we laugh, we cry, we struggle. We get angry and frustrated. We are overjoyed and in tears simultaneously. We love in ways that are sometimes completely insane, and we reach for each other…. we reach for our girl friends. In doing so, we reach for a better tomorrow, while we learn to make the most of today.

To steal a phrase from Jackson Browne's *Everyman,* I wanted to create the "everywoman" in Jo and Gina. I wanted my readers to be able to identify with their life experiences. To read about one of their predicaments and say "Ah, yes. Been there done that."

I needed to be able to write about things, events and people that I was comfortable with. In my writings, although none of these characters are real, they were created from many of my own life experiences, interactions, thoughts, and beliefs. I needed to write in ways that provided a connection between myself, my work, and my readers.

I am a woman, so I wrote about women.

I have lived life and made mistakes, made the best of it and moved on. So have Jo and Gina.

As I wrote about their low moments, I cried. As I wrote about their funny escapades, I laughed. I want my readers to feel those same emotions. I want them to walk away from the story of Jo and Gina empowered as a woman, with hope in their heart and joy for tomorrow!

Below, I've included the Old Irish Proverb in its entirety. I hope it brings all of you as much inspiration as it always has to me.

> *Take time to work, it is the price of success.*
>
> *Take time to think, it is the source of power.*
>
> *Take time to play, it is the secret to perpetual youth.*
>
> *Take time to read, it is the foundation of wisdom.*
>
> *Take time to be friendly, it is the road to happiness.*
>
> *Take time to dream, it is hitching your wagon to a star.*
>
> *Take time to love and to be loved, it is the privilege of the gods.*
>
> *Take time to look around, the day is too short to be selfish.*
>
> *Take time to laugh, it is the music of the soul.*

Women of the Ozarks,
Scrapbook Series…

Book X, A Prequel

NATALIE R. VICE

Can friendship last a lifetime?

Everyone says that hindsight is 20/20. If that's true, how much of that image in the rear view affects who we are today, or who we will become tomorrow?

Jo Felsenthal and Gina Ingram were the closest of childhood friends back in Polk Ridge, Arkansas. Growing up in this beautiful, close-knit Ozark community, they were surrounded by love and laughter.

But as these girls grew into women, choices were made, and life took them in very different directions.

Now, they're just hours away from a reunion several decades in the making. A out-of-the-blue Facebook "friend" request has snowballed into a face-to-face meeting. Both women are dealing with mixed emotions—excitement, nostalgia, and more than a little apprehension.

In *Memories of Tomorrow*, Jo and Gina weave their way through childhood memories and difficult life choices. They ponder how to cross over all their yesterdays to the girls they once were. Can they find anything in common after so many years spent living such different lives?

If you like The Sometimes Sister and Hurricane Season, you'll love the *Women of the Ozarks Scrapbook Series.*

Book One

NATALIE R. VICE

Two separate paths. One enduring friendship.

Jo Felsenthal and Gina Ingram were girls of the '60s and '70s and grew into young women during one of the most turbulent social times in American history. The cultural forces of those tumultuous times had a tremendous impact on the choices they made and the women they became. As these two women, now in their fifth decade of life, look back to see just how far they've come, they long for the friendship they once shared.

Having traveled the world for nearly forty years as a military officer and NSA liaison, Jo Felsenthal is now forced to take a step backward and return to her childhood home of Polk Ridge, Arkansas. Stepping back into this old (and mostly forgotten) territory comes with its challenges. Her mom's health is failing, her career and personal life are in freefall, and she hasn't connected with anyone in Polk Ridge in a lifetime.

Gina Phillips has spent a lifetime facing more adversity than she cares to recall. From teenage mom, to widow, to social worker, she has made her way and her life in Polk Ridge, one of the poorest towns in one of the poorest counties in Arkansas. So when Gina decides unwind on her back porch after work, she's more than surprised when a familiar, yet long neglected friend pops up in her Facebook feed. Yet there she is: Jo! Gina's dearest childhood friend—now a complete stranger—is back in town. Her quick click on "friend request" is about to have lasting consequences....

Can these women find a way to bridge a lifetime of separation and recapture the friendship of their youth? They'll soon find out if a bucket full of childhood memories is enough to reignite a once-treasured friendship long abandoned. Set in a beautiful, close-knit Ozark community, *Tomorrow's Promise* is a story of family and friendship. Through joy and despair, Jo and Gina will walk you down a nostalgic road and perhaps into a promising future. If you like The Book Club and The Summer Girls, you'll love the *Women of the Ozarks Scrapbook Series.*

How Much of Your Future Depends on Your Past?

After decades apart, childhood friends Jo Felsenthal and Gina Ingram spend their first summer together after more than forty years. A few weeks spent revisiting life as the girls they used to be and getting to know each other as the women they've become has shown them that time and circumstances have changed them both.

They're different women with different ideals and different convictions. Gina has spent her life in their hometown of Polk Ridge, Arkansas, nestled in the Ozark mountains as a counselor for the poor and drug addicted. She's sympathetic and open minded to others' hardships. Jo, by contrast, has lived her life in the military—an environment with a single-minded purpose and a demand for rigid discipline.

For Jo, blending back into a community that distrusts the very government she has spent her life defending, leaves her completely at odds with the people Gina seems to adore. When Jo meets Gina's friends Max and Maxine, she's thrown for a loop as these two conspiracy driven hippies challenge her beliefs about the government and law—all of which has shaped her into the woman she is today. Her instant dislike of Gina's friends suddenly threatens the newly reunited childhood friends.

In *Crossing Yesterday*, the second book in the *Women of the Ozarks Scrapbook Series*, Jo and Gina are forced to ask: Just how far apart can two people be and still find common ground?

If you like Beach House for Rent and The Book of Lost Friends, you'll love the *Women of the Ozarks Scrapbook Series*.

Book Three

It's the stuff you *don't* see coming, that changes your life's path.

Throughout your life you learn to plan, prepare, and plan some more. You learn to cope with the expected. It's the stuff you don't see coming that can be your undoing. Jo Felsenthal and Gina Ingram's lives are no different.

When Gina's son has a child out of wedlock and she learns that her deceased husband also fathered an illegitimate child, her carefully constructed family life is turned inside out. Gina's longtime friend and sometime boyfriend Melvin, suddenly seems completely uninterested in her latest turn of events. If she has ever needed a friend, it's now.

Jo has her own set of issues. She's confronted with revisiting her feelings for Paul Collections, the high school sweetheart she couldn't make room for all those years ago. Jo also finds herself confronted with a sister that seems to be in the midst of a mid-life crisis and co-workers in the midst of a blossoming romance.

In the *Unraveling,* life's plans seem to be quickly dissolving. They had a path they wanted to follow. They were making careful preparations for that path. Now, it seems that everyone and everything is conspiring to turn the most carefully constructed plans upside down! How did it all get so complicated?

Suddenly, finding a lost friendship seems like the easiest part of their lives.

If you like Before We Were Yours and The Sisters Café, you'll love the *Women of the Ozarks Scrapbook Series.*

Book Four

Recapturing love and a sense of adventure isn't as freeing as you would think…

Ready to take advantage of retirement, lifelong friends Jo Felsenthal and Gina Ingram plan a two-week trip to sunny California. In this new environment, far from home, the two women finally feel free to say and do what they want. Gina finds she's rather fond of pot and Jo re-discovers her love of wine. They finally understand the phrase, *California dreamin'*.

What was supposed to be a short trip, turns into months away from their home in the Ozarks. Gina begins to feel the increasing tug of her responsibilities at home in Polk Ridge, but is reluctant to leave her never-ending vacation in the Golden State.

Jo, on the other hand, has finally come to the staggering

revelation that she's once again fallen in love with teen sweetheart Paul Collections. This time, though, Paul isn't necessarily a free man.

As realities in their hometown of Polk Ridge, Arkansas keep calling, Jo and Gina find themselves trying to answer an age old question: Is the grass really any greener on the other side?

If you like The Sometimes Sister and Beach House for Rent, you'll love the *Women of the Ozarks Scrapbook Series.*

Book Five

NATALIE R. VICE

The Fates giveth, and the Fates taketh away…

Almost a decade has passed since a fateful Facebook friend request brought childhood friends Jo Felsenthal and Gina Ingram back together after a life apart. The inseparable girls of '76 are now older, wiser, and best friends again. They've shared tears and laughter, anger and happiness, trials and triumphs. They have stopped searching for the girls they used to be and found lasting friendship in the women they have become.

Jo has rekindled a once-lost love and Gina has reconciled herself with life in the Ozarks. The girl who once had no idea which path to choose, has found that the path has chosen her. The mountains, the people, and the family Gina has fought so hard to hold together have given her the sweetest gift of all: enduring love.

Jo and Gina's friendship has been tried and tested for almost half a century. Together, they have experienced girlish dreams and desires, love and loss, happiness and regrets. But most importantly they've grown into women who cherish a lasting friendship.

Then fate deals their enduring friendship one final blow...

Wait For Me, is the fifth and final book in the Women Of The Ozarks Scrapbook Series, and will share the poignant final stories of two women who have seen so much and found friendship through it all.